PAINT IT RED

# PAINT IT RED

## PRIMARY PALETTE MYSTERIES, BOOK I

## JESSICA MEHRING

Five Bears Press

Colorado Springs, CO

Cover photo: Maddy Baker

Five Bears Press

6510-A South Academy Blvd. #121

Colorado Springs, CO 80906


Paint It Red / Jessica Mehring. — 1st ed.

ISBN 978-1-7354013-2-4

*For Jeremy: Until the stars burn out.*

# PROLOGUE

———————

My blue Jeep Wrangler sailed south on the highway, the desert wind nudging from behind, bringing me ever closer to Santa Fe. Through the open windows I could smell sun-warmed sagebrush and pine. I was happy to be back—this time, for good. I hoped.

Open plains gave way to rolling hills dotted with adobe homes. As I drew closer to the city, spiky yucca plants were slowly edged out by bright yellow rabbitbrush, gnarly Gambel oak, and shapeshifting juniper. The late morning sun was a white orb in an azure sky—without a cloud in sight, it was a blank canvas.

As I drummed on the steering wheel to the beat

of the electronic dance music streaming through my speakers, I glanced in the rear-view mirror. A patrol car was coming up behind me—fast. I checked my speed and cursed my music choice. Club music helped keep me awake on the road, but it also made me drive faster. As much as I wanted to get to Santa Fe and settle into my new life, I couldn't afford another speeding ticket.

The lights on the patrol car flicked on and the siren whooped twice, signaling me to pull over. I steered the Jeep onto the graveled shoulder of I-25, and for a moment I couldn't see the patrol car in my mirror through the cloud of dust.

I rifled through my glove compartment for my registration paperwork and jumped a little when the officer knocked on my window.

I didn't even have time to hand the officer my license and registration before he crooked his finger at me and said, "Ma'am, I'm going to have to ask you to step out of your vehicle."

"Is something wrong?" I asked. My heart pounded in my chest. Other than the odd traffic citation, I'd never been in trouble with the law. I couldn't imagine what was making this officer suspicious of me. "Was I speeding that much?"

"Please step out of the vehicle, ma'am," he repeated.

I stepped out. The officer motioned toward the back of the Jeep. My heart raced faster.

As we rounded the bumper, the officer pointed at the thick red fluid dripping off my bumper and pooling on the ground beneath it.

"This has been dripping from your vehicle for at least a mile," the officer said. "Looks like a blood trail."

I gulped audibly.

"But I've seen enough blood to know that's not blood," he finished.

Red paint was dripping from the bottom of the tailgate, over the chrome bumper and onto the gravel under the Jeep.

I let out the breath I had been holding and laughed loudly. "Desert Rose Red," I said. "It's a can of Desert Rose Red—left over from a mural I did in Chicago."

The officer chuckled. He had a lovely, slightly crooked smile. "Thought it might be paint. Good to know my detective skills are still on point."

I opened the tailgate. It seems the last time I had closed the tailgate, it had smashed the gallon can of rusty red paint up against the edge of a metal toolbox. The dent had been enough to pop the top off.

"Well, hopefully there's a good detail shop in Santa Fe. My poor Jeep's a mess!"

"Sparkle Pro is the best. Tell them Officer Goodson sent you and they'll throw in a free air freshener." He hooked his hands on his belt loops and rocked back on his heels.

"Officer Goodson. Got it." I looked at his badge. *New Mexico State Police.*

He beamed at me and nodded his head toward the south. "You're only about an hour out, but they only do detail jobs on the weekend. You got anything you can use to sop up the paint? It's making a mess of the highway, too."

"I'm an artist. Of course I do." I leaned over the pile of belongings in the back of my Jeep, trying my best to avoid getting red paint on my jeans. After moving a few items around, I pulled out three folded and stained towels and made quick work of wiping up the spilled paint.

"You artists are better than boy scouts—er, girl scouts. Scouts, period. You always come prepared," he said.

"You know a lot of artists?" I closed the back of the jeep.

He shrugged. "I grew up in Santa Fe."

"That must have been nice," I said wistfully.

"Clearly you don't know many other artists," Officer Goodson said.

Suddenly a red Porsche flew past, kicking up enough desert dust to make me cough.

"Gotta go," the officer said, tipping his campaign hat in my direction before he bolted back to his patrol car. "Duty calls. Best of luck in Santa Fe!"

# CHAPTER ONE

----

"This painting is breathtaking," I said to the stern old woman who stood next to me. "It looks a lot like...but it couldn't be..."

Mrs. Eleanor Valencia wore her gray hair in a tight bun at the nape of her neck. She nodded sharply at the large landscape painting that hung over the fireplace in her Spanish Pueblo-style home. "It's an original Alejandro Navarro," she said. "He was a friend of the family."

"You're kidding me," I said without thinking.

She turned her dark, hawk-like face at me and I winced.

"I do not kid. This piece is my pride and joy," she said, reaching up and caressing the worn wood frame. Her whole demeanor seemed to soften when she touched it. "It is called El Camino de Rosas," she said with a gentle sigh.

"I remember now. I recognize this painting," I said in awe. "It was in one of my college art textbooks."

Turning to me once again, but with a kinder countenance since gazing upon the Navarro painting, she said, "Shall I show you your new home?"

"Yes please!" I said, unable to hide my enthusiasm, though peeling myself away from the work of art before me was a testament to my willpower.

Bianca had sent me pictures of the Little House—the small cottage behind the main house that Mrs. Valencia lived in. If it were half as delightful in person, I would be over the moon.

My new landlord took me through the back door. A tall coyote fence ran along the right side of the back yard. Along the left side was a dirt driveway that ran the length of the yard and seemed to wrap around the small adobe house at the back of the property. We wound our way through a thick but well-tended garden toward that small house, and my legs felt weak from excitement.

We stood in front of the bright blue door of the adobe cottage and Mrs. Valencia turned the key in what looked like a shiny new lock.

Her hand on the doorknob, she stopped and turned to me. "Absolutely no men." The old woman's eyes turned dark and she pointed one crooked, wrinkled finger at my slack-jawed face.

Composing myself, I responded, "That won't be a problem, Mrs. Valencia." After my breakup last month, I had no interest in meeting men. It was time to put myself first, for a change.

Mrs. Valencia's face softened ever so slightly at my response. She nodded.

I followed close behind as she led me into the Little House, the cottage I would be renting from her. The rust-red Saltillo tiles on the floor felt solid and well-worn under the heels of my equally well-worn ankle boots. The interior walls were a softer shade of beige than the ruddy exterior adobe, and delightfully reflected the light coming in from the large windows on two walls of the living room.

This was going to be an amazing place to paint.

As I walked around, Mrs. Valencia stood in the

center of the small, one-bedroom house, her spotted hands folded serenely in front of her. I ran my hands along the edge of the faux-marble counters in the tiny kitchen. Smooth and squeaky clean, those counters had clearly been installed recently. This house was a dream come true. Situated on the opposite end of the lush yard from the main house, it was a very private space—and it was only four blocks from the plaza in downtown Santa Fe. It felt too good to be true.

"How come this place is vacant?" I asked, my eyes roving over the large living room that would double as my studio. "I mean, it's incredible." I chose not to voice the rest of that thought: *And the rent is really cheap.*

Mrs. Valencia's well-lined face stretched into a prim smile. "It *is* incredible. I agree. The young woman who lived here before decided that she didn't want to pay her rent anymore." She cleared her throat. "I do not tolerate bad business."

My father's face flashed in my mind. "I do not tolerate bad choices," he had said before cutting off payments toward my college tuition. I nodded at my new landlord. She had a difficult personality, I could already tell—but I was used to dealing with difficult personalities.

I walked into the back bedroom, leaving Mrs. Valencia standing like a stuffy statue in the living room. My feet sank into the thick cream-colored carpeting. The west-facing window was shrouded by sheer white curtains that let the late summer sun come through in a dreamy haze. The room itself was just big enough for a queen-sized bed and a dresser, with not much space to walk between. When I opened the closet door, however, that no longer mattered. The walk-in closet took up the full north wall, and the front half of it had floor-to-ceiling wire shelving.

"My husband, God rest his soul, renovated this house for his mother." I jumped at the sound of Mrs. Valencia's voice so close behind me. "She had a lot of shoes."

"This will be great for storing my art supplies," I said, pushing down on one of the shelves to test its strength.

"Yes, that's what the former tenant kept here as well. And it's why we had to re-carpet this entire room." The old woman's lips pinched together into a foreboding frown. "I might warn you that if you get paint all over this house like she did, you will lose your security deposit."

"Yes, Mrs. Valencia," I said, feeling the strange urge to curtsey. "I understand." *Note to self, put plastic sheeting down...everywhere.*

I was scared to ask, but I couldn't stop myself. "Would you be okay with me painting the walls if I paint them white again before I move out?" This place was perfect—too perfect. It needed a pop of color. Or twenty.

"Absolutely not. If you need color, add it here." Mrs. Valencia waved to my bleached blond hair, turned on her heel and walked back out the bedroom door.

I stood there in shock, not sure how offended I should be. After a moment, I shrugged and grimaced to myself. She did have a point. I bleached my straight, shoulder-length hair for a reason—to experiment with some new colors. Unfortunately, my life had turned upside-down before I got the chance to get to the salon.

I caught up with my new landlord in the kitchen.

"Bianca tells me that you've known each other for many years, and that you've visited Santa Fe in the past—so I'm sure I don't need to tell you this, but water is very precious here in New Mexico." She waved her hand toward the slender chrome faucet in the kitchen sink. "You are responsible for paying your portion of the utilities, so you will pay for what you use." She folded her hands in front of her again and turned her head to stare out the small window over the kitchen sink. "Please, be thoughtful. My family has been in this land for generations. It's an extraordinary place full of extraordinary people." She turned back to me. "Take good care of it and it will take good care of you."

A loud noise from the direction of the main house made us both jump. Mrs. Valencia muttered something under her breath. She turned to me, "The renovation crew must be here earlier than I expected," she said. "You'll have to excuse me. Here is your front door key and a spare. Park your car around the back—there's no garage, but you have private parking behind the Little House. Come find me if you have any questions."

When Mrs. Valencia walked out of the house, I pushed the lapis-blue front door—the only real color in the place—closed behind her and leaned against it. I had never lived in such a nice place before. Everything smelled new. Even the keys in my hand glistened in the sunlight coming through the windows.

Back in Chicago, every place I lived was old and worn. Floors creaked and windows leaked. I never minded, though, because every place had history and character. I wasn't sure what character the Little House had yet—it wasn't obvious through the renovations. Not yet, at least. But by the time I was done with it, the Little House would have enough character to fill a book.

I walked over to the window in the small alcove off the kitchen. Through the fruit trees, neatly trimmed bushes, and flower beds, I could barely see the main house. *That* house had the kind of history and character I was expecting in downtown Santa Fe. Worn adobe walls curved softly around brightly painted doors and windows. Someone there had an eye for color—but based on her response to my question about painting the walls, I doubted it was Mrs. Valencia. Maybe her husband was the one with the artistic streak.

When Bianca—my best friend from college, a local boutique owner and the reason I came here—called to tell me about this place, she mentioned that Mr. Valencia died three years ago. His wife has been living here alone ever since. Bianca seemed to think Mrs. Valencia could use the company.

Today I had gotten a distinctly different impression. The old woman seemed quite capable of handling life on her own.

My cell phone vibrated in the back pocket of my jeans. I pulled it out and looked at the caller ID. Speak of the devil. "Hi Bianca."

"So? What do you think? Are you *in love*?"

My eyes swept the empty house. "I do love it. You were right. It's perfect."

Bianca squealed. I pulled the phone away from my ear. "The moving truck should be here tomorrow. I'm going to head over to the hardware store for some cleaning supplies here in a minute. I had a little accident with a can of red paint on the drive down. The back of my Jeep looks like the scene of a murder."

"Oh no. Well, Phil's over on West Alameda is probably the closest hardware store to you. Phil, the owner, usually runs the register. You'll love him," Bianca said.

"No. No, no, no. You're not starting that already, are you?"

"Starting what?"

"Trying to set me up. Because I told you, after my breakup with Alex, I am *done*..."

"Eww. No. Phil is just a nice old guy. He's lived in Santa Fe since the 60s. He knows everyone, and he's a good person for a newcomer like you to know."

"Sorry," I said. "I guess I'm feeling a little sensitive." *Way to overreact, Ali.*

"I guess!" Bianca said. "I wish you'd tell me what happened with Alex. I feel like there's more to the story than just a bad breakup."

My heart clenched in my chest. "Someday," I said. "Right now, though, I need to get those supplies, then I need to bring my stuff in from the Jeep before it melts in this heat. Is it always this hot in August?"

It took a moment for Bianca to respond. I took it that she was upset. "Okay. And yeah, in the eight years Rocky and I have lived here, there was only one August that didn't get above 90 degrees at least once."

I wasn't ready to share what happened back in

Chicago. It was still too raw. But Bianca deserved more openness from me than I was giving her. She had been nothing but kind, supportive and generous since I called her sobbing one night in July.

"I'm sorry," I said. "I didn't mean to just dismiss you like that. Look, I know this whole thing is weird. I've been down here to visit you five times since college, and now all of a sudden I'm moving here," I started.

"I invited you here," she said.

I sighed. "Yes, you did. And I'm so grateful for that. I honestly didn't know where to go, but I knew I couldn't stay in Chicago, and there was no way I was going to move in with my parents in California. You threw me a lifeline when you helped me relocate here." I felt myself tearing up. I pulled the phone away from my ear and shook my head to clear it. "My heart has been put through a meat grinder. I will tell you the whole story—soon. Right now, though, I just want to get settled in and start my new life here." I took a deep breath and waited for Bianca's response.

"Okay. I understand."

I was relieved at her simple answer. "And this

place is in *desperate* need of some color, so I'm anxious to start hanging up some artwork!" I said, trying to lighten the mood.

"Well, when you're done with what you need to do today, our couch will be ready and waiting. A pitcher of margaritas will also be ready and waiting," Bianca said. I could hear the smile in her voice and I breathed a sigh of relief.

"You are a godsend, Bianca. I'm going to need that margarita after the drive down here," I said. "I got pulled over by state patrol about 45 miles outside of town. Apparently, my broken paint can was turning I-25 into a Jackson Pollock painting. The upside was that the officer was *really* cute."

§

Later that night, I sipped my stiff margarita from a pink twisty straw and admired Bianca's back patio. The lattice pergola was lit up like Christmas with fairy lights and tiki torches.

"The only thing that's missing out here is a giant blow-up Santa Claus," I joked.

Bianca stuck out her pink-painted lower lip. "Hey now. I did the best I could to make this feel festive and sufficiently artsy for Santa Fe. It's not my fault my police officer husband is paranoid about burglars." She sipped her margarita and glared at me.

"Why don't you get a dog?" I twisted the flamingo-pink straw in my unmanicured fingertips. It was a really good margarita.

"Rocky is allergic," she said. She followed the statement with a long pull from her blue twisty straw. "I love dogs. Remember that dog I adopted in college?"

"Adopted?" I laughed. "You mean found on the side of the road. Yeah, I remember Bingo. I also remember how devastated you were when he died."

Bianca pushed her long black hair over her shoulder and sighed. "He was so perky. Who would have guessed he was already 18 years old when I found him?"

"He was a sweet boy," I lied. I remembered six months of total destruction when Bianca took that scraggly little mutt in. Her apartment wasn't safe for my purse or my shoes until that little tornado died quietly in his sleep one night. She was surprised to learn that he had died of old age. I was surprised he hadn't died from ingesting something he shouldn't have.

That was one of the things I loved most about Bianca—and it was the same thing that always drove me crazy about her. She sees the best in everyone.

A light breeze stirred the warm night air, bending the flames of the lit tiki torches. I sat back in the low Adirondack chair and breathed it in. There was something about the smell of the high desert that made me feel at peace. Crickets chirped softly, and a smattering of stars dotted the black sky.

I heard the sound of the sliding glass door opening behind me and turned. Rocky stepped out, bottle of beer in hand. "Hey ladies. Ali, the couch is all made up for you."

Bianca's husband was exactly what you would expect—or hope for—from a Santa Fe Police officer. He was six-feet tall and well-muscled, but not too beefy. His dark brown hair was cut short, with the sides shorn so close to his head you could see his scalp. His dark eyes were confident and compassionate. And in the nearly nine years I had known him, he had raised his voice only once—when he had tried to stop a texting teenager from walking into oncoming traffic.

"Thanks, Rocky. I really appreciate you guys letting me crash here tonight. It's frustrating having a place to live but not having my *bed* in it yet." I said, slurping the last of my drink. "Of course, after this margarita, I could probably sleep on a cactus just fine."

Rocky smiled and raised his bottle. "Bianca makes a mean margarita. It's one of the many reasons I love her. And you are always welcome here, Ali. You know that."

"Well, I appreciate it, nonetheless. How come you're not indulging in one of these fabulous margs with us, Officer Romero?"

"I've got an early morning," he said. "Besides, I'm planning to fill my margarita quota this weekend." He gave his wife a wink.

Bianca shot daggers at him with her eyes. She caught me looking at her and flushed.

"What's going on, you two?" I demanded.

"Nothing!" They both said at once.

"Ugh. I forgot. You don't miss a thing." Bianca put her drink on the low iron table on the other side of her and crossed her arms.

"I have an eye for detail. It's what makes me a good portrait artist," I said matter-of-factly. "Like I noticed your nails are freshly done. And your house is sparkling clean. And while you are a gracious host, you are *not* a perfectionist—so what gives?"

Bianca and Rocky exchanged a look. Rocky shrugged.

"Well," Bianca started, "We were going to make it a surprise, but..."

"Spill it," I said, getting annoyed.

Bianca turned her whole body toward me and flapped her hands up and down like a bird. "We're hosting a welcome-to-the-neighborhood party for you tomorrow night!" She squealed.

"Oh, you guys are so sweet!" I said. I stood up and gave them both hugs. "You really didn't have to go to all that trouble. I'm happy just to be here."

"Your buddy here thinks it'll be good for you," Rocky said, tilting the mouth of his beer bottle at his wife.

Bianca beamed at me, radiating that infectious joy that had made it so easy to stay friends for so long, even from across the country. "I think this will be a good way for you to get to know some people around here."

I smiled and nodded. "I'm looking forward to it," I said truthfully. "I'm glad you told me, though, because I would have been furious if I'd shown up in paint-stained yoga pants."

# CHAPTER TWO

———

When I stepped out the door of the Little House early Friday evening, I couldn't help but notice the contrast between the disaster area that was my box-strewn living room and the tidy garden that lay just outside the door. Even in the late summer heat, the garden burst with life. Colorful flowers and fragrant fruit trees were weeded and pruned, with neatly trimmed juniper bushes separating sections of the large yard.

Mrs. Valencia stood watering a bed of snapdragons, her white blouse and long floral skirt swaying in the light breeze. She looked up as I shut the door.

"Goodnight, Mrs. Valencia!" I shouted over my shoulders as I locked the door behind me.

"Goodnight, Ms. Porter," she said. "Be careful tonight. There's trouble in the air."

I stopped in my tracks and turned around. She was looking down at the flowers, still watering the same spot as if she wasn't really paying any attention to what she was doing.

"Everything okay?" I asked.

"Fine, dear," she answered shortly. When she looked at me, I could see a few strands of hair had escaped her bun. She looked a bit wild that evening in the garden.

I smiled tightly, not wanting to push because I hardly knew her, but also feeling like something was very off with my landlord. Shrugging off the prickle at the back of my neck, I walked around the side of the Little House and started the Jeep.

§

Bianca had transformed her backyard from Christmas to Las Vegas rooftop. There were lights wrapped around every bush and tree, draped along the fence line, and bordering the small shed at the far end of the long yard. It was dazzling—and the sun wasn't even down yet.

I sipped my first margarita of the evening, feeling like I had earned it. The movers had arrived late that morning, and to make sure I had enough time to get ready for the party, I did my fair share of hoisting furniture to hurry things along. My back was aching something fierce, but the workout made my arms look extra toned in my sleeveless red dress.

"You look stunning," Bianca said as she sidled up to me. Her dark brown eyes roved the yard, surveying the few people who had shown up on time. As if answering my unspoken question, she shrugged and said, "We're on Santa Fe time here. People show up when they show up." She sipped what looked like lemonade from a tall glass. "And hey, it means more limoncello for me!"

"Wait, there's limoncello?" I said, elbowing her in the ribs. "You're holding out on me!"

"I saved you a glass. It's our last bottle from our anniversary trip to Rome last year. I only break it out on special occasions. You being here is a very special occasion." Bianca put her arm around my waist and leaned her head on me. "I'm so very glad you're here. Especially with these *guns* on you. You could put down a riot with those arms!" She poked my arm.

"I had a pretty strict workout routine back in Chicago. Gotta keep in good shape to run a creative department during the work week and be on my feet painting portraits on the weekends."

"Are you still planning to pursue a full-time painting career here in Santa Fe?" Bianca asked, her eyes earnest.

"That's the plan. Of course, I need to find some clients first..." I started.

"Oh YAY! I'm so happy to hear that," Bianca cut me off. "Felicia!" She called to someone over by the buffet table on the patio. "Come here for a sec."

A petite woman with dark hair in a low bun turned and made her way over to us. She held a small plate in one hand and reached the other hand out to shake mine. "You must be Alissandra," she said.

"This is Felicia Barnes. She owns Southwest Treasures, a fantastic gallery over between the plaza and Canyon Road." Bianca said to me as I shook the woman's small hand.

Felicia had a firm, warm grip.

"Everyone calls me Ali," I said, smiling at her. She looked like she had stepped out of a painting. Her bronze face was fine-boned yet strong looking, and her smoothed-back black hair was so glossy it almost glowed.

Felicia nodded serenely and popped a cheese cube in her mouth.

"Ali here is one of the best portrait artists on the planet. She's open for new clients," Bianca said, beaming. "Will you keep your ear to the ground for us?"

Felicia's dark eyes bored into mine. It felt like she was taking a peek inside my soul for a moment. She might have been six inches shorter than me, but I had the compulsion to step back. I held my ground, though, and she held her gaze. Bianca looked at me, then at Felicia, then back at me. After a moment, Felicia's eyes softened and she asked, "Do you have photos of any of your work?" She jerked her chin at the small purse I had put on the bistro table behind me.

"I do," I said. I pulled my phone out of my purse and showed her a few recent projects.

Felicia took my phone from my outstretched hand and began flipping through. I winced inwardly and prayed I didn't have any embarrassing selfies in my digital gallery.

"Interesting," she said, handing back my phone. "You've got an eye for capturing emotion. I will keep you in mind the next time someone at the gallery asks about wanting their portrait painted."

The sound of breaking glass echoed through the darkening evening. "I'd better go see what that's about," Bianca said before she dashed off.

Felicia continued to pick at the food on her plate, watching me out of the corner of her eye. "You're living in the Little House at Villa Valencia, right?"

I nodded and smiled. I liked that the place I was staying had a *name*.

"Keep your nose clean. Mrs. Valencia isn't forgiving."

I opened my mouth to ask her to elaborate, but Felicia turned and walked back to the buffet table before I could make a sound.

"Man. That tiny woman sure can put away some canapes." A deep and somewhat familiar voice came from right behind me.

Startled, I spun around to see who was speaking.

The man was taller than me by about five inches,

putting him around six feet in height. His dirty blond hair was cut in a tidy military fashion, slightly longer on top, and created a perfect frame for his hazel eyes. At the end of his blue-flannel-clad arm, he held a margarita glass with a purple twisty straw.

"It's you!" I said. "The cop who pulled me over on my way into town."

"It's me," he replied. "But I prefer 'state police officer' to 'cop.'"

The man's smile threatened to melt me where I stood.

"What are you doing here?" I said, my manners taking a back seat to my shock.

"Rocky is an old friend of mine. And Bianca makes the best margaritas, so I never miss one of their parties." He laughed. "I'm Ben Goodson." He put out his hand. I shook it gingerly. His grasp was firm but not *too* firm. I could tell a lot about a person from their handshake—and most men unconsciously try to crush the other person's hand. It's the lizard brain's way of establishing dominance. Ben's grasp showed well-controlled strength.

"Well I suppose I should thank you again for not

giving me a ticket," I said with a laugh. "Because this would be even more awkward if you had."

"I don't feel awkward at all," Ben said. His eyes crinkled up at the corners when he smiled, and I found myself staring.

I closed my eyes tight and opened them again to clear my head. Suddenly I noticed a lot more people at the party. It was as if I had been in a bubble talking to this strikingly handsome officer (this time without the embarrassment of having just painted two miles of I-25 red).

Bianca came swooping back, her long white skirt swishing around her ankles. "Oh good, you met Ben!" She waved her hand toward him. "You can thank him for the extra festive light situation we've got going here tonight. He was here all day helping Rocky make my yard look magical."

I shook my head and grinned at her. "I met Ben yesterday morning, actually."

Bianca looked at me quizzically.

I freed her from her confusion. "He's the cop—sorry," I looked at Ben and smiled, "*state police officer*—who pulled me over."

She smacked Ben on the arm with a loud crack.

"Why are you harassing our lovely newcomer? Way to make her feel welcome in Santa Fe."

"OW," he said, rubbing his arm where she hit him. "I pulled her over because she turned I-25 into a Picasso painting."

Bianca turned to me, again looking confused.

"Remember the spilled paint in the back of my Jeep?" I asked.

"Aaaahhh. Yup. Okay, Ben, you're forgiven. But only because you didn't ticket her." She looked around and seemed to notice the same thing I had—the yard had filled up with people mingling under the darkened sky and twinkling lights. "Oh wow—so many people I want to introduce you to, so little time. I need to play hostess for a bit, but I'll be back with new names for you to memorize."

Just before she walked off, Bianca turned toward a small gap in the fence, squinted and frowned. "Ben, we might have an unwelcome visitor," she said.

Ben and I both looked in that direction and squinted to see in the dim light. All I could make out was a quick movement in the gap in the fence, then no movement at all.

"I think she's gone," he said. He took a big sip

of his margarita. "I'm not in the mood for this tonight."

"When *are* you in the mood to be stalked?" Bianca asked. She laughed, took a swig of her drink and walked toward a group in the far part of the yard.

"Sorry about that," Ben said. Between the dance music now coming from the house and all the people who had arrived, the party was getting noisier, and I could barely make out what he said. My confusion must have shown on my face, because he continued to explain. "There is an artist here in town who has been stalking me. I went out on one date with her and I knew it wasn't a good match. She disagreed."

"Do you have a thing for artists?" I asked with a sly smile.

"What?" he said loudly.

I shook my head. It was too loud where we were standing. I touched his arm, then pointed toward the apple tree back by the shed. He nodded back.

We began to make our way to what I hoped was a quieter part of the yard when I heard Rocky's voice calling my name. I turned and saw him waving violently at me to come over to him.

Begrudgingly, I held up a finger to Ben to let him know I would be just a minute, then wove my way back through the crowd to Rocky.

His face was ashen.

He walked toward the house and I followed. He didn't stop in the house, though—he continued walking all the way through the front door and across the street. My heart was pounding.

He finally stopped and faced me. It was much quieter here, and I was glad because what he said to me was not something I would want him to shout at a party.

"Mrs. Valencia has been murdered."

# CHAPTER THREE

————

"You can't go in there yet, Ali," Rocky said, putting his arm across the open front door of Villa Valencia's main house. I got on my tiptoes and tried to look past him through the azure doorframe. All I saw of the living room were the backs of unfamiliar heads.

"How was she killed?" I asked, rocking back on my kitten heels and passing Rocky an innocent look.

He grabbed my arm and all but dragged me down the flower-lined front walk and out to the curb next to his unmarked black Dodge Charger. When we finally came to a stop, Rocky released my arm and said, "The only reason I told you what happened is because you live here and you might have some insight into what happened."

"I have literally lived in this town for two days. I don't have any...Hey, who's that?" Across the small front yard and through the big front window of the house, I noticed a tall, well-dressed man fondling the El Camino de Rosas with white gloves. These were not the same latex gloves the police were using—even from a distance, I could tell they were cloth from the bright white color.

Rocky turned to look, his brow still furrowed. "That's Aaron Taylor," he said. "He's the art consultant for our precinct."

"What's he doing with the El Camino de Rosas?"

"The what?"

"The painting. *That* painting." I pointed. "It's famous." I didn't wait for Rocky to answer. I tried to push past him. Rocky grabbed me by the shoulders and held me in place. "Please," I begged him. "That painting is a historic artifact—and it's obscure enough that I'm not sure your consultant will know just how valuable is. Please let me go talk to him and make sure he knows to be careful with it." I stared into Rocky's eyes, unblinking, hoping he could see the importance of this.

"I'm going in with you. You are not to touch a *thing*. And if you see anything at all that might help us solve this case, you are to tell me immediately." He set his jaw. "Do we have an understanding?"

I nodded, my heart skipping.

Rocky took my elbow and led me through the front door. Just as I crossed the threshold, I saw Aaron running a wet cotton swab over a corner of the famous Navarro painting.

"Hey!" I said to the tall, brown-haired man. "What are you doing?"

Rocky elbowed me and shook his head in warning.

Aaron Taylor turned up his nose and lowered his eyebrows. "I'm doing my job," he said, his deep voice condescending. "Who are you?"

Two uniformed police officers looked up from their conversation across the room and stared right at me.

"She's with me," Rocky's voice boomed in the small space.

In that moment of distraction, my attention

shifted from the painting before me to what stood just beneath it: A massive pool of blood.

The thick puddle of blood lay between the living room and the kitchen. It was heaviest near the fireplace over which El Camino de Rosas hung, and trailed off toward the kitchen. A hammer rested next to the blood, the head on the floral area rug that covered the living room floor, and the handle on the tile leading to the kitchen.

I felt lightheaded. Rocky must have seen me go cross-eyed because he quickly put his arm around my waist to hold me up. "Time to go," he said, guiding me back toward the door.

"No!" I shook my head to clear it. "No, I need to talk to him about that painting!" I said, pointing back at Aaron over my shoulder. I tried to peel myself out of Rocky's grip, but the two police officers who had been eyeing me just a moment before came over and helped him walk me out of the house unceremoniously.

"What were you thinking causing such a ruckus?" Rocky fumed as we stood on the front lawn. "This is an active crime scene. The murder weapon is still on the floor, for God's sake, and you were about to pass out on top of it." He crossed

himself and looked at the sky. "Forgive me, Lord."
His eyes returned to my face.

He nodded to the two cops who had dumped
me on the lawn with Rocky. They returned to the
house, leaving the two of us alone on the thick
grass. I'd never seen him so angry.

Rocky pointed a finger at me. "Not only are you
putting the integrity of this investigation at risk,
but now I'm going to have to explain to my wife
why I throttled her best friend."

I crossed my arms. "That painting is incredibly
valuable. Not just monetarily, but historically. I
wanted to make sure no one was messing with it."

"Taking care of valuable artwork is literally what
Aaron does for a living. He's a prominent art
broker and agent here in town."

"And I wouldn't harm a fiber on that canvas,"
Aaron said as he strolled up to us on the front
lawn. "The investigators wanted a blood splatter
sample, and I offered to get it for them because I
know how to do it without damaging the painting.
You're welcome."

Inwardly I cringed. The man radiated arrogance.

"I've been trying to get my hands on the Camino
for years," he continued with a sigh. "Mrs. Valencia

wouldn't even consider selling it to me. Such a shame. It could have been the crown jewel of my client's collection. Instead it was..." he waved his hand dismissively at the adobe house, "...here."

I squinted my eyes at him in the darkened yard, sizing him up as best I could. "And how convenient. Now she's not here to say no to you anymore."

Aaron looked at me coolly. "First, I considered Mrs. Valencia a friend. I wouldn't dream of pursuing the purchase now, out of respect. And second, there is blood splatter in the lower left corner of the painting. While there are some macabre collectors out there, none of *my* clients would find that appealing." He pulled on the crisp cuffs of his white sleeves and smoothed the front of his khaki slacks.

"Mmhmm," I said, crossing my arms. "And where were you tonight?"

"Ali," Rocky said sharply, elbowing me in the ribs.

I bit back a yelp of pain. *That man is stronger than he realizes.* "What?" I responded. "He just admitted to wanting to get his hands on Mrs. Valencia's priceless Navarro masterpiece."

"Not priceless," Aaron corrected. "Extremely high-value. And if you must know, I was at Gallery 329 hanging pieces from a client's collection for a new show." He turned to Rocky and said derisively, "You can check the security cameras." Aaron looked me up and down. "Now if you don't mind, I am going to dinner."

He turned his back abruptly and walked away, practically sauntering across the lawn to his white SUV.

*That's odd. He's wearing two different color socks.* He didn't seem like the kind of guy who would do that purposefully.

"Satisfied?" Rocky asked me, his thick arms crossed over his chest.

"Not remotely," I answered. "My landlord is dead." I took a deep breath. "I don't suppose you'd let me go back in and take a look around?" I knew the answer before he said it, but it was worth a shot.

"Not a chance," he said firmly. "But you might want to go home and make sure everything is all right." Rocky nodded at the gate on the side of the house.

I nodded and started to walk that direction. I

stopped and turned back to my friend's husband. "I'm sorry if I caused any trouble. I've been told I'm...inquisitive."

"You mean nosy? Yeah, I know you're nosy," Rocky said with a slight smile. "Just let us do our jobs. We'll figure out who did this, and we'll keep you safe."

I don't know why, but until that moment, it had not occurred to me that I might be in danger. A chill washed over me and suddenly the night was very dark.

I wound my way through the fruit trees in the back yard and reached my small house. The only light came from the half-moon in the black sky and the neighbor's back porchlight. I pulled my key out of my pocket and fumbled for what felt like minutes to open the front door.

I flipped on the two lights on the switch just inside. The light from the chandelier over the dining nook lagged behind the lamps in the living room, but in a split second everything was visible.

Nothing looked out of place at first glance. I walked through each room, and as far as I could tell, no one had been there.

Satisfied, I went into the closet and pulled out

a large sketchpad and a box of colored pencils. I took them into the living room and set them on the small rug in the center of the room. Then I got to work.

I sketched out in detail the scene that I had witnessed in the main house of Villa Valencia that night. I drew the pool of blood that ran like a slow river away from the fireplace. I drew the painting that hung over that fireplace, potent in its color and history. I drew Aaron Taylor in his khaki pants, white gloves, and mismatched socks.

I leaned back against the couch, admiring the finished drawing. I tapped the end of a red pencil against my temple. *What was missing?*

It came to me in a flash. The blood droplets on the corner of the painting. I added some red to the drawing. Now the scene was complete. On paper, at least.

# CHAPTER FOUR

———

The sound of my cell phone ringing startled me. I looked around, not remembering where I was for a moment. My aching back reminded me that I was sleeping on my old blue couch in the living room of my new home. A home I wasn't sure I'd have much longer. I rolled over and grabbed the phone off the floor next to me after the third ring and looked at the screen. "Hi Bianca," I said into the receiver, my voice hoarser than I expected.

"Are you okay?" The panic in her high-pitched voice was palpable.

"I'm fine, considering. Poor Mrs. Valencia. Who would do something like this?" I got up from the couch and made my way into the kitchen, which, like the living room, was still full of boxes.

"That's a pretty long list," Bianca said. "An easier question would be who *wouldn't* do this."

"What do you mean?" I asked, searching through boxes for my coffee maker. *Bingo.* I found it in the third box, right next to a can of generic grounds that would do just fine this morning.

"She had a lot of enemies," Bianca continued.

"Like who?"

Before Bianca could answer me, someone knocked on the door. "Hey, I'll come over later and help you clean up from the party. You can fill me in then. Someone's at the door." I ended the call and slipped the phone in the pocket of the sweatpants I barely remember changing into the night before.

I looked through the small, frosted window in the door. A partially balding man looked straight back at me with a deep scowl.

"Can I help you?" I said to the stranger through the door.

"Open the door," he said. "I'm the owner."

My heart skipped a beat. A new owner? That was fast. Too fast.

And I'd lived too long in Chicago to trust a stranger at my door.

"The owner is dead," I said. "And I'm armed. Who are you?"

"Tom Valencia. I'm Eleanor Valencia's son," he said. "Now open the door." His voice was as gruff as his visage.

Everything in me wanted to respond with profanities—but I was also not in a good position to get kicked out of my house. "Put your ID up to the window," I demanded.

The man rolled his eyes, but complied, pulling his ID out of the wallet in his back pocket and holding it where I could easily see it through the tiny window.

Satisfied enough, I opened the door a crack. "I wasn't aware Mrs. Valencia had a son."

Tom wore a blue-checkered, sweat-stained, button-up shirt tucked into wrinkled khakis. It looked like he'd been sitting in a hot car too long.

"I wasn't aware she had a new tenant," Tom said, wiping the beads of sweat from his brow with the back of his hand. "So we're even. Who are you, and what happened to Kathy?"

"I'm Alissandra Porter. Who is Kathy?" I asked,

one eye looking at the angry man through the cracked door.

He was my same height, around 5'7", and his frame was slight yet doughy. He looked like he couldn't bench press a cereal box, but he had a paunch that made his shirt bulge over the brown leather belt that held up his pants.

"The woman who lived here before you. What happened to her?" Tom demanded.

"I don't know," I said. "I just moved in two days ago. All I know about the woman who lived here before me is that she didn't pay her rent."

He frowned, the line between his eyebrows growing deep enough I wondered if it reached bone. "My mother didn't mention that," Tom said.

"When was the last time you talked to your mother?" I asked.

"That's none of your business," he spat back.

"A strange man is pounding on my door at the crack of dawn on the day after my landlord is murdered, and he's asking me questions about things I don't know. I feel entitled to ask a few questions of my own." I opened the door wide and stepped out, causing Tom to back onto the patio quickly enough that he almost ran over my lilac bistro table.

Tom's wide eyes indicated surprise, but he quickly schooled his face back into an angry scowl. "The only thing you're entitled to," he said, balling his fists at his side, "is 30 days' notice, according to your lease."

"Your mother hasn't been dead for 24 hours and you've read my lease?"

"I *wrote* the lease that my mother uses—used. I'm a lawyer."

My stomach dropped. In my experience, lawyers were trouble.

"Let me guess. You're an artist, right?" He didn't let me answer. "She always had a soft spot for artists. It's why she discounted the rent, to give artists a leg up in this cutthroat town."

"Yeah, I..." I started.

Tom raised his hand and shook his head, cutting me off. "I don't care. I want to be done with this place. The police want me to stay in town during the investigation, but I just want to get back to Albuquerque, and far away from this ridiculous town. Unless you know something that can help the police find out who murdered my mother in her own home, all you are to me is a strange woman with an attitude." He crossed his arms and glared.

"I don't have an—"

He cut me off. "In fact, the way I see it, my mother was fine until *you* arrived." That statement hung in the air between us.

I opened my mouth to speak, but nothing came out. Was he really insinuating that I might have had something to do with Mrs. Valencia's death? I had been in Santa Fe for *two days*!

I finally found my voice, and all I wanted to do was end this conversation. "I had nothing to do with your mother's death. And I really wish I could help you. Your mother seemed like a great person. I'm sorry for your loss." I stepped back inside the house and put my hand on the door. "Now if there's nothing else you need, I have to get dressed. I have somewhere to be."

"We're not done, Alissandra Porter," he said coolly. "I'll be back." With that, he spun on his heel and stormed back down the gravel path to the main house.

I closed the door and slumped to the floor. My first few days in Santa Fe were not going well.

§

When I arrived at Bianca's house, I heard music coming from the back yard. I made my way around the side of the house and let myself in through the half-overgrown gate.

My dear college friend was dancing around the patio with a broom, lip-synching to "Girls Just Wanna Have Fun". She spun, her long, dark hair swinging like a stole around her shoulders. When she saw me standing there, she gave a little gasp.

"You scared the heck out of me!" Bianca said, putting her hand over her heart.

"Don't mind me. I'm just watching the show!" I said.

We both doubled over with laughter.

"Man, I needed that," I said after we had both caught our breath.

Almost instantly, reality caught up with me and my laughter turned back into melancholy. I plopped down on one of the teal Adirondack chairs, and Bianca sat in the fuchsia one next to it. "You wouldn't believe my morning."

"It can't have been as bad as last night," Bianca

said, her eyes softening. "This is *not* the welcome I hoped to give you."

"Unless you killed my landlord in the ten minutes you left my side last night, this isn't your fault." I stared down at my chipped red nail polish. Even my slapdash home manicure wasn't faring well so far in Santa Fe. "Speaking of murder suspects, you said Mrs. Valencia had a lot of enemies. Who were you talking about?"

"How do I put this nicely so I'm not speaking ill of the dead?" Bianca asked herself out loud. "She was...a woman of conviction. She spoke her mind. Often not very tactfully. She was also a third-generation New Mexican—her home and much of her art collection are incredibly valuable, and there are many people who wanted to get their hands on what she had. She was proud of that, and not kind to people who came looking to buy."

"I understand she had a soft spot for artists," I prompted.

"I would agree with that, from what I knew of her. She was a regular patron of my boutique, a fixture of the downtown art community, and she was also a long-time member of the Santa Fe Plaza Art Association. I only just recently joined the

SFPAA—even though I'm not an artist, the art community heavily influences my business, so it made sense to join once my boutique had found its feet. From what I picked up at the few meetings I went to, Mrs. Valencia's family has always been patrons of the arts. I wonder, though, if she was also an artist herself. She just had that look in her eyes. Like you had when I visited you in Chicago."

That statement felt like a shot to the heart. "I'm not surprised you could see it in my eyes. Being a creative director left me zero time to paint, and sometimes it was physically painful to not be doing what I loved. I thought working in a creative capacity in a marketing and advertising agency would be enough to scratch that itch, but it didn't even come close." I sighed, feeling like that job was years ago—but it had only been a month since I packed up my desk. "Back to Mrs. Valencia, though. So she was kind to artists, but not so much to other people?"

"Let me put it to you this way," Bianca said. "At the last SFPAA meeting, Birdie Lemon asked Mrs. Valencia if she'd considered her offer yet...and Mrs. Valencia dumped a glass of water on Birdie's head."

I stared dumbly. "There's so much in that statement to unpack. First, what kind of name is *Birdie?*"

Bianca laughed. "She's a commercial real estate developer from the East Coast. Wealthy New-Englander who married into an equally wealthy family here in town."

I closed my eyes and shook my head. "Okay, and Mrs. Valencia *dumped water on her head?*"

"Felicia told me the story later. Supposedly Birdie made an offer on Mrs. Valencia's property. Birdie had an eye on that block for a health and wellness complex. Her last project was a huge bust, and she was putting all her eggs in that basket. She was desperate, and Mrs. Valencia wasn't budging—so the tension was pretty high between those two."

I frowned and sat back, processing all this new information about the woman I knew for two days before she was murdered in my own back yard. "Speaking of people getting their hands on her property, Mrs. Valencia's son paid me a visit this morning."

"Tom?" Bianca asked.

I nodded.

"How was he?" she asked.

Bianca's face expressed a kindness that I was sure mine hadn't when Tom came knocking. I felt a stab of shame at that.

"I'm not sure how to answer that," I said, shrugging. "He wasn't happy to find me there. He was pretty angry, in fact. I, uh, wasn't very nice to him, though."

Bianca sucked air through her teeth. "Not good. He's a lawyer. And he's probably going to inherit Villa Valencia, because as far as I know, he's Mrs. Valencia's only living descendant."

I pouted and crossed my arms. "It was early. He caught me before I had my coffee, the morning after my landlord was brutally murdered a few yards from where I live. And he was rude!"

Bianca put her hand on my shoulder for a brief moment. I let out a big breath. "I know. Not my finest moment." I leaned back in the chair and stared into the yard which just last night was a place of magic and connection. "He kind of accused me of having something to do with the murder."

"What?" Bianca nearly shrieked. "He can't have been serious."

"He didn't come right out and say it, but he did say that his mother was fine until I arrived here. And he threatened to kick me out."

A crow stood in the yard several feet away, staring at me. It cried out three times, as if to portend my doom. The heat of the day was already setting in, and tiny puffs of red dust rose in the air when the crow leaped into flight from the ground where it had been foraging. It was so dry here—drier than I remember from my short visits. It felt like anything exposed to the air in Santa Fe would inevitably shrivel and leave behind only a husk. I could feel my old self shriveling...and at the same time, I could feel a new determination growing in place of what withered away.

I sat bolt upright. "Tom did say, though, that the police want him to stay in town, but he just wants to get back to Albuquerque—and," I curved my fingers into air quotes, "'unless I know something that can help the police find out who murdered his mother in her own home...' What if I could find the murderer? He wouldn't kick me out if I were the one who found out who killed his mother. Right?"

"Ali, don't. Do you remember the tuna can

investigation in college? You were nearly kicked out of the dorm." Bianca shook her head fiercely.

"I found out who threw that giant can of tuna off the east tower, though, didn't I? I'm pretty good at solving mysteries." I chuckled, tucking a lock of my stick-straight hair behind my ear. A sudden flash of memory stopped my laughter abruptly. My stomach turned at the image burned into my mind of Alex's foot sticking out from under the covers of our shared bed as I rounded the corner into the bedroom. "At least, I used to be good at solving mysteries."

Bianca must have seen my face fall because she put her hand on my shoulder again and squeezed. "This isn't like trying to find the culprit behind a college prank. This is a murder investigation. And Rocky would be *pissed* if you got involved—he might not be a detective, but he still works with those guys. He was so mad when he came home last night, he watched CNN to calm down. *CNN*, Ali."

"He doesn't have to find out," I said, looking directly into my friend's dark brown eyes. "Does he?"

"I don't like this," she said, her lips pinched.

"You can help me," I prompted. "It'll be like old times."

She shook her head. Her dark hair fell like a curtain around her face.

"I like it here. But I can't afford to live here if Tom kicks me out. The low rent on the Little House is what made this move possible. If I find his mother's murderer, Tom could get back to his life in Albuquerque. He'd be grateful." *Hopefully grateful enough to leave me be.* I pinched my lips together and took a deep breath through my nose. "You don't have to help me," I said, resigned to Bianca's refusal, "but will you please not tell Rocky?"

It was at least a minute before Bianca turned her face to me, looking up through the curtain of hair. "I'll help you. I don't like this, but I don't want you doing this by yourself."

I wanted to jump up and pump my fist in the air, but I held myself together and simply said, "Thank you. I owe you one."

"You owe me a lot more than one, Ali. And you can start by helping me clean up this mess of a yard."

# CHAPTER FIVE

———

Everything hurt as I pulled my Jeep into the narrow alley that ran alongside the main house and around back to the Little House. Emptying overflowing trash cans, picking up discarded bottles and napkins, taking down the string lights—I was amazed at how much we had to clean up that morning. Especially since the party ended early. Apparently, word of the murder spread quickly after I left. People didn't stick around long at the party after that.

I parked the Jeep and took Ben's business card out of the cup holder. Bianca had given it to me as I was leaving her house.

I thought back to the conversation as I turned the card over in my hand.

Bianca's eyes flashed with barely contained excitement. "Ben asked me to give it to you, and told me to have you call him," she said.

"I don't think that's a good idea," I answered, holding the card gingerly. "The last thing I need right now is to get involved with a man."

Bianca frowned. "He's a good man."

"I'm sure he is. But I'm not a good woman. Not right now," I said.

Now I sat in the driver's side of my Jeep, staring at the coyote fence in front of me. My ex's betrayal had broadsided me, and I hadn't recovered. After the fact, all the signs were there. But somehow, living with him every day and even working in the same building, I had missed all the clues that were right in front of my nose.

It was ironic, really. Alex was an art insurance adjustor, and, among other things, he taught me so much about how to spot inconsistencies in people's stories. Combined with what I learned from him about art crimes, and my own knack for observation, I am the last person he should have been able to fool. My love for him had made me blind.

I wouldn't make that mistake this time.

This time, I would see the clues. I would find the patterns. I would solve this crime.

The sound of two men shouting snapped me out of my reverie. I looked through the passenger side window toward the main house, where the sound seemed to be coming from, but I couldn't see anything through the trees.

I got out of the Jeep and stopped only long enough at the Little House to drop my purse and Ben's card inside the front door. Then I wound my way through the garden toward the back door of the main house.

There was crime-scene tape across the storm door at the back of the house, but I could see Tom standing at the back of the house, toward the alley side. As I approached, I saw him point his finger toward the face of a shorter, rounder man.

"Three thousand dollars is a ridiculous amount of money for your shoddy work," Tom yelled, swinging his finger toward the kitchen window. "Even if the bill were my responsibility—which it's not—I wouldn't pay it."

"My work is excellent! And the bill *is* your responsibility. If you own this house, now, you pay for the work," the other man shouted back. He had one hand on his hip and the other pointing to the same place Tom was pointing.

"My mother hasn't even been buried yet, and you come here looking for a handout..." Tom started.

"I have subcontractors to pay. The job is done, and I need to be paid for it." The other man's voice, instead of getting higher as I would expect in an argument, got lower and more menacing. "Until you pay me, I still own these materials. I will rip them out of this house with my bare hands if I have..."

"Everything okay?" I said as I walked up, suddenly feeling like I needed to break up this fight.

"This is none of your business," Tom spat, turning his red, hawk-nosed face in my direction.

"I'm David Ramirez, Mrs. Valencia's contractor," said the shorter man. "I'm trying to collect payment for the last job I did for her—and *this* man is insulting me."

"She didn't pay you because you did a shoddy job," Tom returned fire.

"She didn't pay me because she was *cheap*," David said, balling his fists.

"How dare you say that about my poor dead mother!"

"There was nothing poor about that woman except her soul."

Tom swung at David and caught him on the edge of his jaw as David attempted to duck. Both men were rendered off-balance—David fell into the side of the house and Tom stumbled forward, tripping over a sprinkler head and landing face-down on a bed of asters.

David righted himself quickly, but Tom took a moment to turn over in his flowerbed landing pad. I stood behind David and grabbed the hose hanging on the side of the house. I unreeled it and put my hand over the faucet, ready to hose them down if they started up again.

As Tom flipped over on the ground and turned his face in our direction, I burst out laughing. Fully half of his face was smeared with what looked like poop. David must have noticed the same thing because he burst out laughing just a second later.

"I will sue you for everything you've got, David," Tom growled from the ground, propped up on his elbows now. "This is assault." His lip curled into what I'm sure was supposed to be a nasty snarl, but caked in poop-colored mud (oh, how I hoped there was manure in the mix, too), it was hard to take him very seriously.

"I'll see you in court, then, Tom," David said, still smiling. "Santa Fe courts don't take kindly to crooks—or smug Albuquerque lawyers." With that, he carefully walked around Tom, through the side garden and out the front gate.

Tom and I were left alone in the back yard, and the silence was deafening. Until Tom broke it. "What are you looking at?" he hissed at me.

"Here, let me help you with that mess," I said. I cranked the faucet on and aimed the hose at his face.

§

"Know anyone who's looking for a decent portrait artist?" I asked Bianca on the phone. It was now Saturday evening and I was sitting at the small round table next to the kitchen in the Little House. "I need to make some money *fast*."

"What's going on?" she asked.

"I've got one week to find a new place, pay the deposit and move."

"Is Tom selling the property?"

"I don't know."

"Then why do you have to move out?"

"Tom just posted an eviction notice on my front door. I...may have sprayed him in the face with a hose when I got home today."

"Ali! What were you thinking?"

"Honestly, I wasn't thinking." I stood up and began pacing the living room. "When it comes to men like him...Bianca, I lose my mind. He was just acting so vile—toward David, toward me—I just felt so angry. He was laying there covered in mud, I had the hose in my hand, and I just...snapped."

"Is this because of what happened with Alex? Did he do something to you? Physically?" Bianca's voice was soft.

I stopped in my tracks. "No. No. Alex was a piece of work, but he never did anything like that to me. He just..." I took a deep breath. "I caught him in bed with my assistant."

Bianca gasped.

"Oh, it gets worse. They'd been sleeping together for months, right under my nose. I mean, these were the two people I spent all my time with—Alex at home and Cindy at the office. And you know me, I notice *everything*. I pride myself on seeing the details. That's why I was a great creative director, and why I thought I might be able to make it as a portrait artist. But somehow I didn't see their affair until I literally walked right into it."

"No wonder you're angry," Bianca said. "I'm at the shop going through some new merchandise. Why don't you come keep me company until I'm done, then let me feed you some dinner and pour you a big glass of good wine."

I turned to my right and looked through the window in the breakfast nook that faced the main house. The sun was still high in the sky, but as it slid toward the west it was beginning to cast long shadows over the garden between the two houses. The yellow crime-scene tape seemed to glow in that light, standing out from the beige adobe walls it was stuck to.

I felt out of control. I also felt like I was blowing my chance to make it as an artist here in Santa Fe.

"I need to figure out who murdered Mrs. Valencia," I told Bianca. "It's the only way I'm going to be able to stay here." *And finally move on from my past.*

"Come to the shop. We'll make a plan together," Bianca pleaded.

I smiled at the phone in my hand. "You're a good friend."

"Of course I am," she said with a laugh. "Now let me do my job as your good friend. Get over here."

# CHAPTER SIX

———

The Desert Wind Boutique was tucked into a strip of galleries, jewelry stores and souvenir shops just off the Santa Fe Plaza. Unassuming from the outside, though always with a lavishly decorated front window, the shop was twice as large as one would expect on the inside.

I meandered through the racks of peasant shirts, fringed leather jackets and boot-cut designer jeans.

"May I help you?" An older woman with short gray hair and cat-eye glasses walked up with a friendly smile.

"I'm looking for Bianca," I said. "I'm Ali."

"Oh, Ali!" the woman said, her face stretching into a delighted smile. "It's so great to put a face to a name. She just went to the back—let me take you there."

I nodded gratefully, then followed the woman through the length of the store to the back.

"Through there," the woman said, pointing at a narrow doorway.

"Thank you," I said as I walked through. The scent of leather and soap washed over me on the other side of the door.

Bianca was standing next to an open box of what looked like leather purses, but her attention wasn't on the merchandise. It was on the man she was in a heated conversation with...Ben Goodson.

"Assured me his alibi checks out..." Bianca was saying as I walked up and cleared my throat. Bianca jumped a foot and put her hand over her heart. "Ali! You gave me a heart attack."

Ben's tanned face flushed almost imperceptibly when he caught sight of me. He quickly schooled his expression into a welcome smile.

"Who's got an alibi?" I asked the two of them.

"David," Bianca said.

Ben glared at her. She squinted in a mock-glare right back at him.

"I told Ben here about your little run-in with

Tom and David today. He seems to think the two men might be dangerous. I was reassuring him that David was one of the first suspects Rocky spoke with—you know, because of the hammer at the scene, and there being some renovation work going on in that kitchen. David's cousin confirmed that he was checking on a job site across town."

"Hey, she went home to a *murder scene* last night. I don't think a little concern is unwarranted," Ben said, defending himself against Bianca's chiding. His dirty-blond hair had a bit of shine to it in the spotlight he was standing under.

"Well, I appreciate the concern. But I'm the dangerous one today, it seems. I got a little carried away with the hose." I looked at my feet, shuffling them uncomfortably.

"I'm sure there are a lot of people who would be jealous that you got the opportunity to spray Tom Valencia in the face with a hose," Bianca said, stepping around the open box and moving to my side.

I chuckled. "It *did* feel good. In the moment, at least."

"I have to get going," Ben said suddenly. He locked eyes with me, and my heart stopped for one long moment. "It was great to see you again, Ali." His bright smile lit up the room. "I asked Bianca to give you my number. I hope you'll use it."

I smiled and nodded at him, momentarily dazzled by that smile. *Ali, get your act together! Say something smart. Or funny.*

Before I could get my mouth to work, Ben had walked out of the room and I was alone with Bianca. I smacked the heel of my hand against my forehead. "Ugh. Way to go, Ali," I scolded myself.

Bianca put her hand on my shoulder. "It's okay," she said. "You're out of practice talking to drop-dead gorgeous, single men. The good news is, he likes you. You'll get more practice here soon."

I couldn't tell if Bianca was teasing me or if she was serious. I stared at her with my mouth hanging open.

She burst out laughing. "Okay, that *was* funny watching you go all tongue-tied. But in all seriousness, he does like you. So how about you help me put out these purses, then we can talk about it over a glass of wine."

§

Later, I was once again sitting on Bianca's back porch with a drink in hand. This was starting to feel like a habit. It wasn't a *bad* habit, though. It reminded me of our college days, sitting on the back porch of the old house we rented on The Hill in Boulder. Parties raged in the houses around us, but our house was always a place of peace and quiet.

That's why Bianca and I got along so well from the beginning. We didn't bring our drama home—but when we wanted adventure, we weren't afraid to crash a party.

"Those portraits that you did two years ago—the ones of the corporate executives—do you still have those?" Bianca asked me as we sipped our wine under the fairy lights in the darkened back yard.

"Yeah. No gallery would touch them in Chicago. They're in my closet back at the house. Why do you ask?"

"I heard that Felicia just lost one of her exhibiting artists," she said. "The artist promised three pieces for the opening this Friday, and she just told Felicia today that they won't be done in time."

"Poor Felicia. What's she going to do?" I asked,

taking a sip of the crisp white wine Bianca had handed me the moment I arrived. The chill of the wine contrasted deliciously with the warm New Mexico evening. I took a deep breath and smiled. The smell of sun-warmed earth still hung in the air.

Bianca snapped me out of my trance. "I suggested she exhibit your executive collection—if it was available." She smiled and looked at me sideways.

"What? Oh wow. I wasn't expecting that. I don't know if they're ready. I don't know if they're good enough." I swallowed hard. I had experienced some success with traditional portrait painting in Chicago—commissions, mainly—but my experimental works hadn't gotten any traction with the local galleries.

"Do you hear yourself? Of *course* they're good enough. Those galleries in Chicago didn't know what they were missing."

"The Executive Series paintings were an experiment. I'm not sure they get to the heart of what I was trying to say."

"Let Felicia be the judge of that," Bianca responded. She pointed at me with her wine glass. "Call her tomorrow. I can give you her number."

"She gave me her card at the party," I said, taking a deep breath.

"There you go. No excuse. This could be your big break."

"I sure could use the win. And the money, assuming any of the paintings sell. I've only got enough savings to cover me for a few months at most."

"I have a good feeling about this," Bianca said. "And hey, worst case, if this doesn't work out and you don't sell some pieces before you run out of money, you can come work with me at the boutique."

I laughed. "Do you really want me near your customers? 'Pardon me, ma'am, but that is *not* your color.' 'No, sir, I don't think that leather jacket makes you look slimmer—in fact, I think it makes you look like the cow it came from.'"

Bianca snorted, then winced and put the back of her hand to her nose. "Ow! Wine does *not* feel good coming out of my nose."

We both laughed until we were crying. It felt so good to be here with my best friend on this warm high-desert night with a cool glass of good wine...it was almost enough to make me forget the trouble I was in.

I pulled a lock of my bleached blond hair down in front of my eyes. "I need to do something with this before I step out in public again," I said. "Do you know any good hairstylists?"

"Stan Lieberman is excellent," Bianca responded. "Just don't mention Mrs. Valencia in his presence. He might take clippers to you."

My ears perked. "They didn't get along?"

"The way I heard it, Mrs. Valencia's regular hair stylist was on vacation and she went to Stan for her weekly wash-and-curl. She didn't like the job he did, and she told him loudly. Stan was offended and told her—and this is a direct quote from Rocky's cousin, who is an esthetician at that same salon—'if she wanted to continue to look like a page out of Octogenarian Monthly, she should go get her hair done at the senior center.' An argument ensued and he told her to leave. She did—and then she badmouthed him all over downtown."

"Oof," I said. "Sounds like a customer service nightmare on both sides."

"Mrs. Valencia was a well-respected woman. That cost Stan quite a lot of business."

"Enough to kill for?" I asked, raising my eyebrows.

"I don't know about that," Bianca said. "Stan is a bit of a drama queen, but I can't imagine him *murdering* someone. Murdering their hairdo in a fit of rage, sure—but not taking a hammer to someone's head."

"We never know what people are truly capable of," I said before downing the rest of my glass of wine.

Just then, raised voices wafted from the house to my ears.

"What the heck?" Bianca said, turning around in her chair and facing her house. "Who's here at this hour?"

The voices grew loud enough for me to make out the conversation all the way from the backyard.

"It's not classified, Rocky. You're not an FBI agent. You can tell me," a woman's voice said firmly.

"I don't know anything, Birdie. And if I did, I certainly wouldn't share it with you," Rocky said, his voice rising.

"I'd better go see what's going on," Bianca said, standing.

"I'll come with you," I said, following her into the house.

Rocky was standing in the living room with a woman I could guess by the loud conversation and the even louder yellow pumps to be the famous Birdie Lemon. She stood a few inches taller than me, with legs for miles. Her blue skirt suit was neatly tailored, showing off her small waist and ample bosom. Birdie's golden blond hair was pulled back into a tidy chignon and her makeup was flawless. I was both repulsed by her perfection and in awe of it.

"You might have the city council wrapped around your finger," Rocky growled at the woman, "but this is *my* house."

Birdie remained impressively unfazed. "I'll get the information either way," she said to the formidable man in front of her, "but I was hoping you'd see the benefit of helping me get it a bit faster."

"You can't buy me, Birdie," Rocky said.

She gasped dramatically, putting her hand to her heart. "How dare you suggest I'm trying to bribe an officer of the law!" Suddenly Birdie noticed me hovering in the kitchen.

"You," she said, pointing one polished red talon at me. "You're the woman living in the mother-in-law unit behind Mrs. Valencia's house, right?"

"Don't answer that, Ali," Rocky said, moving his well-muscled form between me and the real-estate queen. Birdie tried to peer over Rocky's shoulder to no avail. "It's time to go," he said, pointing at the open front door behind her.

Birdie eyed the door, then turned back and fiddled with something in her purse. "If you hear any news about what Tom is planning to do with that property, you give me a call. I'll make it worth your while," she said, putting what appeared to be a business card on the credenza by the front door. With that, she turned on her yellow stiletto heel and click-clacked out of the house, leaving the front door wide open.

I made my way from the kitchen to stand next to Rocky in the entryway. Through the open door, I watched as Birdie sashayed down the front walk to a white Jaguar at the curb. Carefully, hoping Rocky didn't notice, I took Birdie's business card off the credenza and slid it into the back pocket of my jeans.

Rocky turned to me and sniffed. "You should just throw that card away now and save yourself the trouble. That woman is bad news."

I blushed at being caught with the card, but the heat faded from my cheeks just as quickly as it had arisen. I'd never heard Rocky speak like that about anyone before, and I was incredibly curious about this woman.

I turned to Bianca, who was hovering nervously in the archway between the living room and the kitchen. She gave me a pinched smile that I took to mean *I'll tell you later.*

"What did she want?" I asked Rocky, who was now shutting and locking the door.

"Information," he answered sharply.

"What kind of information did she think she could get from a cop?" I asked.

"She doesn't care that I'm a cop, just that I'm close to the situation," he growled. "Birdie has wanted to get her hands on Mrs. Valencia's property for years. She was aggressive about it, and Mrs. Valencia didn't take kindly to it. I got called to the house a few times to get Birdie off the property—and the charges never stuck. She's got connections high-up in this town. In my experience, it's better to stay far away from people like her."

"Sounds like a pushy woman," I said, leaning against the arm of the burgundy couch.

"Pushy is an understatement. That woman is ruthless. She'll keep coming until she gets what she wants." Rocky crossed his thick arms over his chest. "Tom's best bet to keep his sanity is to sell that property off quickly—to anyone but her."

*Ruthless, huh? Seems to me like she might be the type of person who kills to get what she wants.* I thought about the Little House—the perfect place to start my new life here in Santa Fe. Then my mind shifted to the incident in the yard with Tom earlier today where I sabotaged my dream. If I was going to move on from my old life and leave the pain in the past, I had to get my act together. I had to fix the situation with Tom. I had to find out who killed his mother so he and I both could move forward at Villa Valencia.

Talking to Birdie Lemon was a good place to start—despite what Rocky might think about it.

# CHAPTER SEVEN

———

The sound of church bells woke me from my slumber, and I regretted it the moment I opened my eyes. My head was throbbing. *Note to self: Lay off the alcohol for a while.*

One hand over my eyes, I felt around blindly with the other hand to find the water bottle I always kept on the nightstand and the painkillers I kept in the drawer underneath. I sat up as much as I could, took the pills and chugged the water.

My head throbbed in tandem with my heartbeat. I laid back on the bed and listened to the church bells while I debated my next move.

The bells must have been coming from the Saint Francis Cathedral on the edge of the plaza. The sound was both reassuring and irritating. The Baptist church I grew up in didn't have bells like that. As a kid, I was always a bit envious of the Catholics for how beautiful their cathedrals were. The architecture, the ornamentation, the music—a Catholic church was a work of art.

A sound much less melodic reached my ears when the bells finally fell silent. Hammering, ripping, and thumping sounds were coming from the direction of the main house.

I got out of bed gingerly and made my way to the window in the breakfast nook next to the kitchen. I peered out through a crack in the sheer white curtains and saw a crew of men going in and out of the main house. The trees obscured some of my view, but from what I could see, the crime scene tape that had been across the back door last night was gone.

"Be careful!" Tom's voice carried across the garden. "Don't damage the doorframe. That paint color will be impossible to match."

*Is Tom prepping the house for sale?* As I stormed toward the front door of my house to see what was going on, I looked down at what I was wearing. After Rocky drove me home the night before, I had fallen into bed in my jeans and fuchsia tank top. My clothes were now both wrinkled and smelly. I hesitated for a moment, deciding between my curiosity and my...presentation.

My cell phone rang, jolting me out of my dilemma. I ran back to the bedroom in time to pick it up on the third ring.

"Ali, this is Felicia. We met at the party on Friday night?" The somewhat familiar voice suddenly brought my career situation back to the forefront of my mind. Tom's shenanigans could wait.

"I'm so glad you called," I said as sweetly as I could through my splitting headache. "I was going to call you tomorrow, actually. Bianca mentioned you might have an opening for some of my work at your show next weekend."

"That's what I'm calling about. I got a good feeling from you the other night. And my instincts are never wrong. Bianca said you might have three pieces ready—and if that's the case, I'd like to see them. Today, if possible. I'm down to the wire."

My heart pounded faster, and my head felt like it was going to split in two. "I might have three pieces, yes. They're...experimental."

"Can you bring them by in an hour?"

I looked at the clock on the wall. It was 9:10 a.m. No time to go get my Jeep. "I'm so sorry, but my car is at Bianca's house. I don't think I could get to you that fast."

There was a moment of silence on the other end of the line, and I thought for a second that I had blown my chance. She finally spoke. "I'm leaving the gallery at 10:15. If you have the paintings at your house, I could swing by on my way to my next meeting."

I let out a breath I didn't know I was holding. "That would be amazing. Thank you! Yes, I have the paintings here. You can park out front—actually, a better bet might be to take the alley around back. There's some kind of construction going on at the main house."

"Construction?" Felicia asked. "Already?"

"Yeah, I don't know what exactly is going on. But I'm going to find out." I said, glancing back out the window.

"Better you than me. I heard Tom's in town. We don't see eye-to-eye."

"I got the sense that he doesn't value supporting the artist community here like his mother did."

"To say the least. If it were up to Tom, artists

would have been paying a premium to live in the house where Alejandro Navarro lived."

I gasped. "Wait. Navarro lived *here*?"

"Yes, he did. Didn't Mrs. Valencia tell you that?"

"No!" I almost shrieked.

"You live in quite a famous little casita," Felicia said. A rustling noise garbled the first part of what she said next, "...be there around 10:30 or so."

Stunned that I was under the same roof where Navarro had lived and painted many of his masterworks, I couldn't seem to form words. I nodded at the phone cradled against my ear.

"Ali? Okay?" Felicia prodded.

I snapped out of my stupor long enough to respond. "Yes. Yes! Thanks, Felicia. I'll be here." *I'll be here soaking up the artistic genius of Alejandro Navarro. Holy cow.*

§

By the time I was showered, dressed, and done with my hair and makeup, it was already 10 a.m. The construction noise continued and was now joined by loud mariachi music. My curiosity would not be denied. After I pulled the paintings out of the closet and unwrapped them in the living room in preparation for Felicia's visit, I stepped out onto the front porch and peered across the garden at the main house. The crew had a radio perched on the step up to the back door, which must have been the source of the music.

I desperately wanted to go over and ask them what they were doing. But I couldn't risk a run-in with Tom when Felicia was going to show up any time. I may be an artist, but I still wanted to appear professional to this kind gallery owner who just might give me my first real shot at being a *full-time* artist.

I sat on the lime green chair next to my lilac bistro table and ran my fingers over the chipping paint on the tabletop. I had found this patio set at a thrift store when I first moved to Chicago after college. Painting it myself had been liberating. For the first time, I truly believed that I could create the life I wanted without my family's support. After my father had cut off payment to the university, I had scrambled to find work and pay my way through to graduation. I pressed forward because I knew a creative career was the right path for me—I was absolutely certain of that. But no matter how certain I was, I still had this voice in the back of my head that sometimes whispered, *What if you're wrong? What if you can't do this on your own?*

Spray-painting that bistro set on the tiny balcony of my Chicago apartment—an apartment I had found and I had paid for from *my* hard work—had quieted that voice for good.

I looked up from my reverie to see a face staring back at me from the kitchen window of the main house.

It wasn't Tom.

I squinted my eyes. Between the distance and the reflection on the glass, I couldn't make out much detail—but I could tell the face was female. She had bangs cut straight across her forehead.

The woman stared at me, unblinking. Like a creepy mannequin.

As suddenly as the face appeared, it disappeared. Even in the growing heat of the late morning, I got chills.

The crunch of gravel drew my attention to the other side of the patio, where the alley led to a parking area behind the Little House. A beat-up old blue pickup truck pulled up.

Felicia exited the truck and came around the

front end, her long burgundy skirt swishing around her legs. I stood to greet her.

"You look like you've seen a ghost," she said as she walked up and embraced me in a warm hug.

I squealed a bit inside. *We're on hugging terms!*

"I don't know what I saw," I answered honestly. "There was a face in the window that I didn't recognize." I chuckled and rocked back on my heels. "Of course, I haven't even been here a week, so that's not entirely strange."

"This property has a lot of history," Felicia said, staring vacantly at the main house. She shook her head as if to clear it. "I'm sorry, dear, but I'm in a bit of a hurry. May I see the paintings?"

I nodded and walked to the front door, waving for her to follow. As we entered the living room, my heart skipped a beat. This was it.

Felicia walked over to the three large paintings I had propped upright against the couch. They were nearly as tall as her. One by one, she stood in front of each painting, her hand over her mouth so I couldn't see her expression.

The paintings were of the three founders of the creative agency I had worked at in Chicago. But only I knew that. These were not portraits in the traditional sense. I had painted what I saw *in* the men—not what I saw *of* them. They were highly stylized images of what I believed to be these men's characters: a referee, an empty power suit, and a meditating man with a bull's head.

Her eyes on the final painting, Felicia shook her head. Her hand moved from her mouth to clasp her other hand in front of her skirt. She turned to face me. "I'm sorry, Ali. These are provocative and outstandingly executed, but they aren't right for my show."

My heart sank. "I understand. Thank you for considering them anyway." It was hard to say those words without crying, but somehow, I managed it. I took a deep breath and tried to clear my swirling head. Maybe my father was right after all. Maybe it was a silly idea to come here and try to make a living through my art.

"Do you have anything else I could see?" Felicia asked with an encouraging smile. Her black hair was pulled back into a low bun, the same as it had been at the party. Standing there looking at me like that, she reminded me of a kindergarten teacher.

I felt pitied. And I didn't like it.

"No, that's it," I said. It wasn't completely a lie.

The other paintings I had on-hand were even more experimental than these three. They weren't even portraits—they were early attempts at painting flowers. If she didn't like these...well, no point in showing her anything else.

Felicia cocked her head and squinted her eyes just the slightest bit. "Okay. If that changes, please let me know. You've got talent. I've got a particular clientele. I'm hoping those two things meet in the middle someday."

I walked her to the door. As we stepped back out onto the patio, I heard Felicia gasp behind me. "Kathy?" she said sharply.

I turned to see what Felicia was looking at. The girl with straight bangs was standing in the middle of the garden behind the main house. Stone still, she stared at me with what seemed like hatred in her black eyes.

Tom stepped out of the back door of the main house. He stood there for a moment as if he were taking in the scene in front of him. "Kathy, leave now," he said, pointing toward the gate to the front yard.

Kathy's jaw clenched. I expected her to argue—or worse, to run at me. Her eyes burned.

In a heartbeat, she lifted her chin in my direction, then turned and walked through the front gate.

I didn't have to be a mind-reader to know that this confrontation wasn't over. I could feel anger radiating from her, even with her back turned to me as she walked away.

By the time I looked back up at Tom, he was gone. The door to the main house was shut, so I could only guess that he had gone back inside.

"Be careful." Felicia's voice startled me. "Those two have black on their souls." With that, she walked to her truck. She stood in the open driver's-side door and said, "I still have a good feeling about you." She smiled slightly, her arm still resting on the door. A moment later, when she got in and drove away, I was left standing alone on my patio trying to process everything that had just happened.

I wasn't alone long.

# CHAPTER EIGHT

———

Just as the sound of crunching gravel died off, it returned. This time it was my blue Jeep that pulled around the back side of the Little House.

Surprised, I walked to the passenger door and peered in. Ben was in the driver's seat. He waved at me and gave me a lopsided grin before turning to open the door.

*I am so glad I did my hair and makeup*, I thought. I immediately chastised myself. *No, it doesn't matter. This isn't going to be a thing.*

"Fancy seeing you here," I said, putting my hands in my pocket so I wouldn't be tempted to shake his hand...or worse, hug him. "What are you doing with my Jeep?"

"That's no way to say thank you, you know." He chuckled, and when his smile reached his hazel eyes his whole face seemed to glow.

Once again, I was mesmerized. And that made me mad. I shook my head to clear it. "Thank you for what?"

"For bringing your car to you. I was over at Rocky's house and saw it parked out front. He told me about last night."

I could feel heat rising in my cheeks and I prayed silently that my fair skin wasn't betraying me by blushing. What did Rocky tell him? That I got drunk at their house after getting evicted?

Mercifully, Ben didn't make me ask.

"So Birdie showed up, huh? She's a piece of work. Please don't let her color your view of the rest of us here in Santa Fe."

The heat in my cheeks subsided. I smiled. "I knew plenty of people like that in Chicago. I know the type. I'm surprised to find it here in New Mexico, but I know the type. She wants what she wants." My eyes flicked to the front passenger-side panel of my Jeep. "What the..."

Ben turned to see what I was staring at. He

stammered, "Uh, yeah. About that. I kind of leaned against your Jeep with my gun belt on."

"Two years and this Jeep hasn't gotten a dent. One day with you and it's all banged up." I ran my thumb over the scratch in the blue paint and gave him the side-eye.

"I'll pay to have it fixed!" Ben said, his eyes pleading.

I waited a breath to respond, just to make him suffer a little bit—though on the inside I was laughing at how desperate he looked in that moment. "There's another way you can make it up to me," I said with a sly smile.

"Anything," he said, his palms raised as if he were begging me not to hurt him.

It took everything I had not to burst out laughing. But this was a serious request, and I needed him to take it that way.

"Help me interrogate Tom Valencia and the woman who lived in the Little House before me, Kathy."

Ben looked at me as if I'd grown a third eye. "Interrogate them?"

"Yeah. You do remember my landlord was murdered, right?" I raised one eyebrow at him.

"Of course. The news is all over NMSP District 1. And Rocky is helping the team working on that case here locally."

"They are both acting really suspicious, if you ask me. And as far as I know, no one has taken them in for questioning."

"The officers didn't need to take them in for questioning. Tom was in Albuquerque when the crime happened—evidence corroborates that alibi. And Kathy..." He shivered visibly. "...she couldn't have done it either."

I squinted at him. "Why couldn't she have done it?"

"Because she was at the party. Same as us."

"I didn't see her there..."

"She didn't *want* anyone to see her there. But she was there. In the neighbor's yard, looking through a hole in the fence. We have the footage from the homeowner's security camera."

"She's your stalker," I stated, putting two and two together.

Ben's black t-shirt pulled across his taught stomach as his broad shoulders moved up and down with a deep breath. "Yup," he said simply.

Suddenly the late morning sun felt stifling. I

moved out of the driveway and into the shade of the patio, crooking my finger at Ben to follow me.

I sat down on the teal chair on one side of the bistro table, and Ben sat in the lime green chair on the other side. I stared at the main house.

"So Kathy, the woman who used to live here, who is now creeping around like some phantom out of a horror movie, is the artist you told me about at the party?" I couldn't meet his eyes. I needed to stay emotionally disconnected from this man and his situation.

"Yes."

"Hmm. Okay." I nodded.

"Okay?"

"Okay. That explains some things."

"You're not...freaked out?"

I looked him in the eye and spoke sharply. "Why would I be freaked out? I don't know you."

His hazel eyes wilted just the tiniest bit. It would have been imperceptible if I wasn't watching closely. "No reason, I suppose."

It was time to change the subject. "Still, though. They're both acting odd. Tom shows up the morning after his mother's death and starts acting like he owns the place."

Ben interrupted, "He does own the place. Probably. Unless his mother disinherited him."

I rolled my eyes. "Semantics aside, it's strange. And Kathy was in the main house today, staring at me out the kitchen window—then she showed up like a ghost in the middle of the yard, again just staring at me. Maliciously, I might add."

Ben's jaw flexed, sending a beautiful ripple up into his cheekbones. "She saw you with me at the party. I'm sure of it. She's probably jealous."

I sat there quietly for a moment, not sure how to respond to that. I didn't want to give him any ideas...but he was probably right. "I have a feeling they know something," I finally said. "Will you help me?"

"Why do you care?" Ben asked bluntly. "You knew Mrs. Valencia for a day. We've all known her for years. Some of us, our whole lives." That statement hung in the air.

I pinched my lips and brushed my hair out of my eyes, unsure about how much I should tell this virtual stranger. I wanted to trust him...this would all be so much easier if I trusted him...but I didn't trust my instincts in that department anymore.

"I love a good mystery," I lied. A light breeze

stirred the air on the patio, but the heat of the late summer day was still oppressive.

Ben frowned at me across the table. "I'll help you," he said. "But only because I want to know what Kathy's up to, too."

"And you owe me for scratching my poor Jeep," I said with a smile.

§

I was doubly glad I had asked Ben for help when I knocked on the back door of the main house and got no answer. A peek in the window and no car parked out front confirmed my suspicion that Tom had left while Ben and I were talking. I had no idea where to find him—but with one phone call, Ben did.

I pulled my Jeep into a parking spot outside a squat, square adobe building on West Alameda Street, turned off the engine and looked over at Ben in the passenger seat. "How were you planning on getting home?"

"What do you mean?" he asked, looking genuinely concerned. "Are you ditching me here? Because I really didn't mean to scratch your car."

His smile was like a rising sun, deliberate and miraculous at the same time.

"When you drove my Jeep over from Rocky's house this morning. How were you planning on getting home?" I asked again. I appreciated all the help Ben was giving me that day—from bringing my Jeep over to helping me get some answers from Tom and Kathy—but I couldn't help doubting his intentions. It was too convenient. And he was too nice. *Alex was nice, too. Nice to me...nice to Cindy...who knows who else he was nice to while we were together.*

"I figured you'd thank me by giving me a lift back to my place. I don't live that far from you," Ben answered, bringing me back to the present.

"You must think I'm nicer than I am," I quipped. With a wink, I turned and got out of the car.

The building was nondescript for Santa Fe. Like most of the small office complexes that surrounded it, Tom's office building was squat, square adobe. There was no sign of the business that occupied it, no logo or name on the door—just a street number above the tinted glass that matched the number Ben had gotten from his colleague at the NMSP. Before I could pull open the heavy wooden door,

Ben reached the twisted iron handle and pulled it open, waving me through.

The small, dank waiting room was empty, as was the reception desk. The only light came from flickering fluorescent bulbs mounted on the low ceiling. I felt like I was in a low-budget horror movie, and I was especially grateful that Ben had agreed to accompany me.

I heard what sounded like metal drawers slamming closed, and it seemed to be coming from the closed door to the right of the reception desk. I turned to look at Ben and noticed his hand was stretching toward his hip, like he was reaching for a gun that wasn't there. We locked eyes and nodded at each other.

We approached the door side-by-side. Carefully and quietly I twisted the doorknob—as I suspected, it was locked. I rapped on the door, expecting the slamming sounds to stop.

Instead, an exasperated-sounding voice called over the continued sounds of drawers slamming, "What? Who is it?"

I opened my mouth to respond, but Ben nudged me and put his finger to his lips. "This is Officer Goodson from the NMSP. I have some questions."

The door flew open and Tom stood there red-faced and scowling, a mess of tipped-over file cabinets and strewn papers behind him. "I've answered enough questions." His eyes flew to my face and he pointed at me. "*You.* I don't have anything to say to you." He turned his back to me and stormed back into the disaster area that looked like it used to be an office.

Still standing in the open door, Ben and I exchanged a glance before we walked through.

"What are you doing?" I asked Tom.

He ignored me and continued to sift through a pile of papers he had gathered on the worn-looking particleboard desk in the corner.

*Well, that's getting me nowhere.* I looked at Ben. He shrugged.

I decided to try a different tack.

"What are you doing to the house, Tom?" I asked. "Getting your money out of it before the police figure out what you did?" Out of the corner of my eye, I could see Ben gaping at me—but he didn't stop me.

Confusion washed over Tom's ruddy face and he immediately stopped what he was doing. "What are you talking about?"

"You've had a construction crew at the house all day. Your mother's body isn't even in the ground yet, and you're already prepping the house to sell it." I said, watching his face for any indication that I was on to something.

Ben elbowed me. "I'm sorry for your loss, Tom," he said kindly. "I can't imagine how hard this has been. And please forgive Ali—she doesn't know your family like I do."

*Interesting.* I filed that tidbit away for later.

He continued, "I just need to know where you were when your mother was killed."

"Same as I've told every cop since Friday night. I was in Albuquerque. I came up as soon as I heard," Tom answered, a little less angry this time.

"And what's your relationship with Kathy?" Ben pressed.

Tom took a quick step back as if he'd been pushed. I took the opportunity to get a good look at the office. It looked like it had been ransacked by a herd of buffaloes.

"Kathy was a friend to my mother," Tom answered.

"We both know that's a lie," Ben said. "But if you'd rather we just go ask Kathy, that's fine. I thought you might want to tell your side first." Ben turned like he was about to leave.

I didn't move to follow Ben right away, but watched first to see if he was bluffing. I was impressed by his firm handling of Tom. This man knew how to take control of a situation, that was for sure. And it was more attractive than I wanted it to be.

Tom ran his thick hand through his thinning black hair and looked at the ceiling for a moment before answering. "I hired her to watch my mom, okay?"

"Now we're getting somewhere," I said.

At the very same time Ben turned back to him and blurted, "So Kathy is *your* fault?"

Tom looked from me back to Ben and then back to me, clearly not sure who to respond to. He finally landed on Ben. "My mother was stubborn, and her health had been failing for years. She would never let me hire someone to help her around the house, much less move her into a senior living facility. And my primary practice is in Albuquerque, so I couldn't be around as much as I wanted to be. Mom had already leased the Little House to Kathy. I just asked her if she'd keep an eye on Mom, and she agreed to it. For a price. Then Mom evicted her...and Mom was there alone again."

Tom stepped backward further into the disheveled office and stumbled into the chair next to the nearly empty desk on the other side of the room. He put his head in his hands, and without looking up, he continued. "I should have been there. I'll never forgive myself." His body rocked with silent sobs.

"I think we broke him," I whispered to Ben.

Tom sniffled, wiped his face with his hands, then wiped his hands on his khakis. I wanted to offer him a tissue, but I had left my purse in the car. He cleared his throat, looking like he was getting himself under control again.

Ben continued in a softer tone. "Kathy stopped paying rent. That's why your mother evicted her. Any idea why she would stop paying?"

Tom's eyes darkened. "Kathy told me that my mother found out she'd been spying on her. I hadn't heard anything about her not paying rent. That makes no sense. With what I was paying her, she was essentially staying in the Little House for free."

"Where is Kathy staying?" I asked Tom.

Tom looked at me impassively.

"Really? The silent treatment?" I said, incredulous.

Ben rolled his eyes. "Okay, children. Tom, where is Kathy staying?"

"There's an artist hostel on East Marcy Street, above the gelato shop. That's where she's been staying, far as I know," Tom answered. "She's been helping me find new contractors to get the house cleaned up, since I don't trust that David guy as far as I can throw him. But we don't chitchat much."

"Do you have her cell phone number?" Ben asked, pulling his own cell phone out of his back pocket.

"She doesn't have a cell phone. Not anymore, at least," Tom said, shrugging. He looked around the room and seemed to notice the mess for the first time. "I came here looking for the agreement my mother signed with that contractor, David. Something is off about that situation. My firm used to use this office to conduct business here in Santa Fe, but we haven't needed it for about two years now. Our clientele has been concentrated in Albuquerque. So right now it's really just a file storage facility for us. I was keeping my mother's files here...but it looks like someone else was here looking for something, too. And now I can't find the files."

"Did you notice anything strange when you came into the building?" Ben asked Tom. Ben's eyes scanned the room.

"Besides the looted file cabinets? Yes, actually. Now that you mention it, this office door was unlocked. These files contain sensitive information, and I would never leave the door unlocked, even with the security system turned on. I thought maybe I had just forgotten to lock it the last time I was here—but now I wonder."

"Does the security system include cameras?" I asked.

Tom slowly moved his gaze from Ben to me and sneered.

Ben asked him the same question. "Are there cameras, Tom?"

His face brightened as he answered Ben. "Only one over the front door. The feed is uploaded to the cloud. I'll have to find the login information."

I was beginning to feel like I was back in preschool. I understood that he didn't like me—and after the hose incident yesterday, I couldn't really blame him for holding a grudge. But I was trying to help. Shouldn't that count for something?

"Get the login and send it to me at this email address," Ben said, handing Tom a card. "In the email, include the day and time you were last here. That'll help me narrow down the window to search in."

Tom nodded.

Ben caught my eye and cocked his head toward the door, an indication that it was time to go. "Thanks, Tom." Halfway through the door behind me, Ben stopped and said to Tom, "Your mother was a special woman. We're going to find out who did this."

# CHAPTER NINE

---

The hostel wasn't far from Tom's office. We could have walked there if we'd wanted to—but I much preferred the air-conditioned interior of my Jeep to the oven dry, high-desert heat. Well, until the silence threatened to smother me faster than the afternoon sun.

"Bianca told me that summers are heating up here, and it wasn't always so hot so late in the year. This is the desert, though, right?" I prodded, looking over at Ben in the passenger seat and hoping for conversation.

Ben grunted.

"Okay, what's going on? You were Super Cop back there, and now you're monosyllabic," I said.

"Don't make me pull this car over." I steered the Jeep into a right turn at a green light and swore under my breath. The lane was closed for construction, and the open lane to my left was wall-to-wall cars. "Looks like I'm pulling the car over anyway. Darn it! This traffic is nuts."

He chuckled. "I was just lost in thought. No need for road rage."

"Penny for those thoughts?"

Ben shrugged. "I owe a lot to Mrs. Valencia. And I don't feel like I ever really paid those dues. Now it's too late. I feel like...if I can help solve this case, it'll balance the scales, I guess."

"Why do you owe her?" I asked.

"Park here," Ben said, pointing to an empty space on East Marcy Street, across from a gelato shop with a chalkboard sign out front that read *Beat the heat with a cool treat.*

Gelato sounded really good, and I realized I hadn't eaten lunch yet. My stomach protested loudly the moment I parked the Jeep and turned the engine off. I clutched my stomach and looked at Ben, hoping he hadn't heard the rumbling. He was smiling from ear to ear.

"Lunch after this?" he asked.

"Yes please," I said with a laugh.

I got out of the car, slung the long strap of my purse over my head and across my chest, and was already across the street before I realized Ben hadn't even opened his door yet. I stood on the sidewalk outside the gelato shop and crossed my arms. He still wasn't coming. I stepped back out into the street, and just as my foot hit the asphalt, the passenger side door of my Jeep opened, and Ben stepped out.

He looked up at the hostel above the shop. His chest rose and fell visibly, and I wondered if he was taking deep breaths to steady his nerves.

Finally, after what seemed like minutes, he locked eyes with me and crossed the street. A small red Honda sedan screeched to a halt and honked loudly, inches from Ben. He grimaced and waved an apology at the driver.

"You sure you're up for this?" I asked when he finally reached my side.

"No. But yes. Kathy is...she scares me," he admitted. "She's like a ghost, haunting me wherever I go. I don't want to encourage her, and I feel like showing up here is going to do just that." Ben's eyes were soft and serious. "I am happy you asked me to help investigate. I'm still not sure why you're involved, but I'm hoping you'll tell me the truth soon."

I gulped.

He continued, "Mostly, though, I'm glad we're doing this together."

The sound of smashing pottery startled me before I could form a response. I jumped a foot in the air and practically landed in Ben's arms.

A rageful scream came from somewhere above me, and I looked up to see Kathy poised to throw another flowerpot at us. Her eyes were black as coal, and her once-straight bangs were sticking out every which way. She looked like a wild animal.

We jumped out of the way before a blue flowerpot joined the yellow one already smashed on the sidewalk less than three feet from where we stood.

"Hey!" Ben yelled. He pushed me under the gelato shop's awning, then ran around the side of the building.

By the time I gathered my senses and ran after him, he was gone. I walked down the narrow alley to the only door. The words *Arroyo Grande Hostel* were painted on a worn white sign to the side of the door.

I turned the handle and was surprised to find the door unlocked. It was so dim on the other side, I couldn't get my bearings right away. I stood in the entryway, praying that Kathy wasn't hiding in the shadows. Once my eyes adjusted, I saw another door to the right marked *Office*, and a set of worn stairs going up.

The sounds of yelling coming from the top of the stairs pointed the way. I took the steps two at a time, running toward the noise.

At the top of the stairs was a long hallway lined with closed doors—save the last door on the right. That one was propped open. I barreled toward it.

I flew into the room in a panic, sure I was running into a fight—but I didn't immediately see anyone. I heard yelling again, and turned my head toward the sound. That's when I saw Ben standing in the open balcony door and Kathy balancing on the narrow wall that lined the balcony.

"Kathy, come down," Ben demanded. He reached out his hand toward her and inched forward cautiously.

Kathy wasn't paying any attention to him. Her

black eyes were locked on me. She pointed at me and screamed, "Her! It's her isn't it?!"

Kathy's face went slack and she drifted backward, like she expected to float on the air.

"No!" Ben yelled, lunging for her.

From where I was standing, it looked like his hand brushed hers as she fell—but he had no chance of catching her.

# CHAPTER TEN

---

It took an hour for the police to finish questioning us. My stomach was no longer rumbling. I was just...numb.

An unmarked police car skidded to a stop near where we were standing across from the gelato shop. Rocky jumped out, pushed his way through the throng of officers, and wrapped his big arms around both Ben and me in one giant bear hug.

"You okay?" he asked as he pulled away. I wasn't sure who he was asking.

"Yeah, we're all right," Ben answered for the both of us. "But Kathy..."

Rocky shook his head. "I just spoke to Nancy at the hospital. Kathy's going to live."

"Oh, thank goodness!" I said, louder than I expected to. I clamped my hand over my mouth, then said in a near whisper. "There was so much blood."

"Head wounds bleed a lot," Rocky said, concern etched on his face. "The fall wasn't that far, but she landed hard. It caused some serious damage, but it wasn't enough to kill her." He frowned at me, his brown eyes shifting from concern to raw curiosity. "What were you doing here, anyway?"

"We just wanted to ask Kathy a few questions about her relationship with Mrs. Valencia." I said.

"Why?"

Ben and I exchanged a glance. Rocky wasn't going to be happy that we were nosing around in this investigation. But I was stumped trying to come up with a reasonable lie.

Ben spoke up and saved me. "I want to help find out who did this to the woman responsible for getting me into the Academy. I knew I was going to have to deal with Kathy, and Ali was kind enough to offer her assistance so I wouldn't have to face her alone."

"This is not your investigation, Ben. The State

Police have no jurisdiction here." Rocky's furrowed brow betrayed his conflict.

"I'm not investigating in any formal capacity. I just want answers." Ben said with a shrug.

"So do I," I added.

Rocky met my eyes. "Let me guess. You think Tom will cancel your eviction if you help solve his mother's murder. Don't think I haven't figured out what you and Bianca are up to."

Heat rose in my cheeks.

Ben turned to me. "Evicted?" he asked.

"He didn't know?" Rocky asked me.

Both men were staring at me and I just wanted to melt into the sidewalk below my feet. I looked back and forth between them, feeling trapped.

Blessedly, my cell phone rang. "I have to get that," I said, turning my back on them and pulling my phone out of my pocket. The caller ID showed Bianca's name. "It's Bianca," I said over my shoulder, knowing neither man would stop me from answering her call.

My head was spinning. I couldn't talk to her right now. I hit the end button, but still pretended I was talking to her as I stepped away from Rocky and Ben. I walked down the street, away from the two men who I knew must be judging me...and rightly so.

I glanced around, making sure no one was moving to stop me. The officers had already taken my statement, but the last thing I needed was to be arrested for fleeing a crime scene. I turned down a residential side street and stopped in the shade of a piñon pine.

Panic rose in my chest. I couldn't go back to the scene of Kathy's near-suicide or face Rocky and Ben. I could walk to my house—it was far, but doable—but that meant leaving my Jeep at the gelato shop. I couldn't afford to have it impounded right now.

I didn't end up having to make a decision. Rocky had followed me.

He walked up to me tentatively. "You're not going to run again, are you?" he said, slowing to a crawl as he approached. The twinkle in his eye gave him away.

I shook my head at him. "I didn't run away." I plopped down on a low rock wall underneath the tree.

"You kind of did. You're lucky you aren't a suspect, because running away in the middle of a police investigation can land you in jail." The twinkle died. "Bianca called the second you left. Obviously you weren't talking to her on the phone. What's going on?"

I took a deep breath and let my shoulders slump forward. "I hadn't told Ben about me getting kicked out of the Little House yet. I'm not exactly proud of that, Rocky. And...I don't know what I'm going to do if I can't figure out a way to stay there." I fought back tears, not willing to give in to this brewing storm of anxiety, humiliation and fear. "I don't have enough money to live anywhere else in this dang expensive town until I start selling some commissioned portraits. And I can't start selling commissions until I know I have a place to live and a studio space to paint them in. I'm just stuck. The last thing I want is for Ben to see me as a broke, desperate, failed artist."

Rocky shifted his gun belt and sat next to me on the wall. "Why do you care so much what Ben thinks of you?" he asked, crossing his arms and cocking his head.

"I don't care what Ben thinks of me," I corrected myself. "I don't want *anyone* seeing me so...desperate."

Rocky huffed. "Ben is a good guy. He's one of my best friends. He's trusting and loyal, and he deserves the truth if you're going to be in his life."

"In his life," I repeated, rolling my eyes. I pushed a stray lock of my hair behind my ear. "Rocky, I just got out of a long-term relationship, quit my job and moved across the country for a fresh start. I'm not looking to be a part of anyone's life right now."

Rocky grinned. "Love happens when you're not looking for it."

"I'm not in love!"

"I wasn't talking about you. But from the volume of your voice right now, I think there's more to this situation than you're admitting to yourself."

I opened my mouth, but no words came out. I glared at my friend's husband and growled.

Rocky slid off the wall and stood to face me. "Look, I won't beg you to go back and talk to Ben. Clearly you need some time to think. I'll drive him back to his house so you can avoid the awkwardness. For now." He squinted his eyes at me. "But you need to deal with this. Okay?"

I nodded, knowing that Rocky wasn't going to let me forget this. He was as stubborn and willful as his wife. It's one of the many reasons he and I always got along so well—he was familiar.

"I'm going to walk to Felicia's gallery," I said, remembering the hope I felt in the woman's presence just that morning. "It'll help clear my head."

"As you wish," Rocky said.

# CHAPTER ELEVEN

---

Southwest Treasures gallery was smack dab between the plaza and Canyon Road, Santa Fe's famous stretch of galleries, sculpture gardens, and art studios. The building looked to be an old house converted into a gallery. The front yard was paved over with multicolored flagstone and enclosed by a low rock wall. Sculptures of desert animals dotted the space, creating a sculpture garden unlike anything I'd ever seen in Chicago. The building itself was pale red adobe, but the wide-open gallery doors were painted white. Red chile ristras hung on the insides of the doors, moving slightly in the gentle breeze.

I walked across the courtyard, weaving between

a bronze coyote and a waterfall with a mountain lion perched atop it. The sun was still high in the sky so early in the evening, and the heat was still unbearable. I prayed the inside of the gallery was cooler than the outside.

I heard a man's voice coming from inside the gallery as I approached the open doors. "About an inch higher," he said.

"Here?" Another man with a deeper voice and the barest hint of an accent spoke this time.

"Yes, that should do it," said the first man.

I walked through the doors into the narrow entryway of the gallery, turned left and rounded the corner into the bigger space beyond. As I entered the room, I heard the sound of nails being hammered into walls. The source quickly became apparent.

Aaron Taylor, the art dealer I met the night Mrs. Valencia was killed, and David Ramirez, the contractor working on Villa Valencia, were standing together against the back wall of the gallery, hanging a large abstract painting.

Aaron must have heard my boots thumping on the worn hardwood floor. He turned toward me, one hand still pensively tucked under his chin. "Oh. You."

*You.* I was getting that a lot lately, it seemed.

"Me," I said. "You get your hands on El Camino de Rosas yet?" I pried.

Aaron turned back to the painting David was hanging. "I wouldn't disrespect the dead like that," he responded, sounding bored. "David, nudge that slightly to the right," he said to the contractor.

"That painting is worth a lot of money," I continued. "Not to mention the historical value of it. Seems to me a lot of art dealers would look past the spiritual implications to get their hands on a piece like that." I knew I was being brash, but this guy irked me. I wanted to irk him back.

"I'm not desperate," Aaron said simply. He clasped his hands gracefully behind his back and turned his whole lanky body to face me. His dark eyes looked me up and down and he tilted his narrow face, seeming to contemplate me. "Why are *you* so interested in the painting?"

"Navarro is one of the greatest American painters in history," I responded. "I did my dissertation on his Red World series. The Camino was in my college textbooks—it's famous. It's a piece of history. And it belongs in a museum, not in a private collector's hands who has no personal connection to the piece."

"Mrs. Valencia had no *personal connection* to the piece," Aaron retorted.

David had forgotten the painting and was now standing to Aaron's left, watching me, his left hand on a credit-card-size silver belt-buckle tucked halfway under his round belly. His hammer was hanging limply from his right hand. A hammer that looked a lot like the one I saw on the floor of Mrs. Valencia's house next to a pool of blood.

"What makes you say that?" I asked. "From what I hear, Navarro lived in the Little House at one point."

"The Valencia family has always been patrons of the arts here in Santa Fe, in one way or another. But that doesn't mean their generosity didn't come at a high cost. Mrs. Valencia comes from a long line of art thieves." Aaron rocked back on his heels as he spoke, never unclasping his hands.

David looked from Aaron to me and back again. He cleared his throat. "I have to go check on my crew," he said. He nodded his silver-flecked head at us and ducked out of the room, back out the doors I just came through.

Aaron and I kept our eyes on each other, neither of us giving David's leaving any attention. It felt like a standoff.

"What do you mean 'art thieves'?" I prodded. "Wasn't the painting a gift?"

"Naïve girl," Aaron sneered. "There's no such thing as a gift in this town. Beatrice Valencia, Eleanor's grandmother, demanded that painting as rent payment."

"That can't be true. When he painted the Camino, he was already well-known as an artist. That piece would have fetched a fortune on the market."

"Yes. It would have. If it had ever left the Valencia property."

"Why didn't he just refuse to give it to her?"

Aaron took a slow breath. "No one refuses the Valencias. It doesn't end well."

"Why?" I asked.

"Ask your friend Rocky," he said.

Before I could respond, a man and two women walked into the gallery. They looked at us momentarily but seemed to be focused on examining the art collection on the wall opposite from where we were standing.

Felicia strode into the room immediately following the group, her long skirt swishing. She had changed her hair since this morning. In place of the low bun, she had braided her hair up over the top of her head. Between her hairdo and her flowing, classical Mexican ensemble, she was only missing a flower crown and she would look like a carbon copy of Frida Kahlo.

She walked toward the three patrons. "Please let me know if I can be of any assistance," she said to them. They nodded their thanks.

Felicia moved gracefully across the floor to me. "Ali, it's lovely to see you!" She gave me a quick hug before addressing Aaron. "Thank you for bringing these, Mr. Taylor," she said to the sour-faced art dealer standing across from me. "And please tell David I appreciate his help, too. I know it was last-minute. I wasn't expecting to sell all three of the Eriksen pieces in one day." She turned to me and winked. "It was a very good day."

"As always, Felicia, it's my pleasure," Aaron said, unsmiling. "I'll be sure to pass along your appreciation to David as well, assuming I see him again before you do."

As Aaron began walking out of the gallery, he stopped short and turned back. He ran his hands down his crisp pink button-up shirt, smoothing invisible wrinkles. "It's the usual percentage. Should those sell, of course."

"Of course," Felicia said with a nod.

Aaron left just as the three customers stepped up into what appeared to be a smaller exhibition room beyond the main space.

Felicia turned to me and shrugged. "I was desperate," she confessed. "I despise working with that man, but I couldn't have so much empty wall space between now and the next delivery. Everything I have in the back is smaller pieces. They wouldn't look right in that space." She looked at the abstract landscape paintings that David had hung for Aaron and frowned. "I don't think they'll sell. But they balance out the wall for now."

Felicia put her hand inside the crook of my arm and guided me to an office in the back, near where the three customers had gone. We had to step up to enter the small room. She tucked her skirt under her and sat in a well-padded leather armchair at an ornately carved desk and waved for me to sit in the antique wooden dining chair on the other side.

From that seat, I could see part of the main gallery through the open door. More people began to trickle in. I glanced at Felicia, expecting her to need to get up and help her customers, but her attention was on me.

I heard a young-sounding woman's voice coming from the direction of the smaller gallery room. "I'll be right with you!"

I turned to Felicia and gave her a questioning look.

She was sitting forward, her elbows on the desk and her hands steepled. "My niece, Rachel," she said simply. "She's been helping out since we extended our hours." Felicia tilted her head slightly, and it looked as if she were trying to read me. It was unnerving, if not entirely uncomfortable. "I want you to know that if the pieces you showed me this morning had even remotely fit the theme of this collection, they would be on the wall out there instead of those...colorful abstracts."

My heart caught in my throat. I didn't know

what to say, so I just nodded. I probably looked like a deer caught in the headlights.

"I'm glad you're here," she said, sitting back in her chair. "I was going to call you tomorrow, but it's nice that I can talk to you about this in person."

"What's going on?" I asked, curious.

"I got a call from a long-time customer this morning, asking if I knew anyone who could do a professional portrait. I don't think you could take much creative license with this project, but if you're open to doing a straight portrait..."

"Yes!" I said, cutting her off. I would paint a portrait of someone's dog right now if it meant a paycheck. "I'd be honored to paint your customer's portrait."

"I'm happy to hear that," Felicia said. "Based on what I saw at the party—the photos from your phone—I think you'd be a good fit for Mr. Lemon's project."

"Mr. *Lemon?*"

"Yes. Lawrence Lemon."

"As in Birdie's husband?"

Felicia gave me a knowing smile. "So, you've met Birdie."

"You could say that," I said. I hesitated to share

anything about last night's run-in with the leggy real estate developer. "She's...aggressive."

"Lawrence isn't like his wife." Felicia said carefully. "He's...Well, just meet him. I think you'll get along. But more importantly, I think he'll like your work."

"If you say so..." I said, feeling deflated.

"He's redesigning the executive offices at his architecture firm and wants a 'proper portrait' for the east wall. At least meet with him."

Rachel's voice emanated from the gallery floor. "Felicia! Can you come out here?"

Felicia glanced at the open office door, then looked at me, her face apologetic. "I have to go. Sunday evenings get busy," she said, the leather of her chair squeaking as she rose. Before she came out from behind her desk, she jotted something down on a piece of paper and handed it to me across the desk. "That's Lawrence's phone number. He'll be expecting you to call."

"Thank you, Felicia. I really appreciate you thinking of me," I said as she swished by.

She turned just as she stepped through the doorway. "I wasn't just flattering you when I said you have talent. I hope you make it in Santa Fe. This town could use a dose of your style."

I stared after the petite woman until she was around the corner and out of sight. My heart was swirling with feelings of both doubt and pride. One thing was for sure, though: I didn't want to let Felicia down.

# CHAPTER TWELVE

It was nearly 7 p.m. when I finally made it back to the gelato shop and my Jeep. The police cars, ambulance and curious crowd were all gone, and my blue Jeep sat alone in the parking area underneath a flickering streetlamp.

The long walk had given me a chance to get my head on straight. I was feeling terrible about ditching Ben earlier. Especially when I thought about how traumatized he probably was after watching Kathy fall off the balcony right in front of him. He probably needed a friend, and I just walked away.

I decided to give him a call before I drove home. I owed him an apology, at the very least. I sat on the bumper and pulled up his number in the contacts list on my cell phone. As the phone rang in my ear, I heard the echo of the ring coming from elsewhere too.

I looked around until I spotted Ben walking up the street toward me, waving his phone. His frame was unmistakable, even in the low light of a streetlamp. Broad shoulders gave way to a narrower waist, giving him a distinct upside-down triangle silhouette.

"I'm sorry," I said as he came within speaking distance. "I freaked. No excuse. I'm sorry." I hoped Ben could see the sincerity in my eyes.

He stood inches from me. I couldn't see the hazel of his eyes in the low light, but the hurt in them was clear as day.

"Rocky told me you left. I couldn't go home." The corners of his mouth turned down just before he ducked his head so I could no longer see his eyes. "I couldn't save her." His voice cracked.

I put my arms around him and willed myself to hold the embrace—even though I was afraid of sending the wrong message, and even though he wasn't hugging me back. I could feel his physical strength in the muscles under my hands, and yet I could feel him trembling too.

"No one could have saved Kathy," I said, squeezing my arms around him tighter. "Except maybe Spider-Man."

He chuckled lightly and his trembling calmed.

I breathed in the scent of him—laundry detergent and Irish Spring soap—and released the hug. I chanced a look at his eyes. The pain in them had softened a bit.

"I wasn't talking about Kathy," he said. He brushed a stray lock of my hair behind my ear. Goosebumps ran down my arms. "Today just stirred up some old memories."

"Will you tell me about them?" I asked. "Over dinner? I'll be getting kicked out of my house here soon. May as well get some use out of the kitchen."

"I'd love that," Ben said, his face warming with a smile.

§

"Cheese or pepperoni?" I asked Ben from the kitchen. "Personally, I'm a pepperoni gal."
He was sitting on the couch, watching me putter

around. "We locals prefer green chile on our pizza," Ben said. His sly grin made me wonder about the truth of that statement. "You know, when you offered me dinner, I thought you were going to cook."

"Bad news, my friend," I said, my head halfway in the refrigerator. I came out with a few cans of soda and a six-pack of Guinness. "I don't cook. But I do have beer. Or whiskey and soda. What's your poison?"

Ben laughed. I didn't want to love that laugh, but it was hard not to love.

"That Guinness is calling my name," he said. He moved from the couch to the small table next to the kitchen and took the Guinness from my outstretched hand. "Anything I can help with?"

"Do you have a favorite pizza place that delivers?" I grabbed my phone off the counter and pulled up the map app, ready to punch in the name of whatever pizza joint Ben named.

"Baron Brothers is great. But I'm paying."

I looked up from my phone. "No, you're not."

"Yes I am. You bought the booze. I'm buying the pizza."

"This is my treat. Please. I was crappy to you this

afternoon. I should have been there for you after what happened to Kathy."

Ben rolled his eyes. "Kathy is going to be fine. Yeah, I feel bad that I couldn't stop her from hurting herself, but I don't blame myself for what she did. And by the way, I'm a state police officer. I deal with people doing crazy things all the time. If you want to buy me a pizza every time something bad happens around me, you're going to go broke in a week." He stood and moved into the kitchen. He was close enough I could feel the heat from his body. "I'm okay. Between Kathy's dumb move and what happened to Mrs. Valencia, it brought up some stuff from when I was younger, but I'm okay. I'm not made of glass, believe it or not."

I squeezed his bicep. "Nope. Not glass." Embarrassed by my boldness, and once again feeling like I was giving him the wrong impression, I stepped back...and slammed right into the fridge. "Ow."

"You okay?" Ben asked, laughing.

"Fine," I said. I pointed to the couch. "Let's move into the living room. I'll call the pizza place."

"Hang on a sec," he said, pulling his phone out of his back pocket. He clicked around on the screen for a moment. "Done. Pizza will be here in 30 minutes."

"Hey! No fair."

"I order from Baron Brothers a lot. It's just easier to use my account on the app. Not a big deal." Ben winked at me.

I sat on the far end of the couch and scowled at him. He sat on the other side and shrugged.

"Well," I said. "We've got a half hour before we're distracted by delicious pizza. Tell me. What upset you so much today if it wasn't Kathy jumping off a balcony?"

Ben's face darkened, and I immediately regretted bringing the question up again. He had finally relaxed, and his even-keeled-yet-happy-go-lucky disposition had returned—and now I'd gone and chased it off again.

"You don't have to answer that," I said, sipping my beer. It went straight to my head, and I realized I never did get to eat today. I hoped the pizza arrived soon or I was going to be flat-out drunk after my first bottle.

"No, it's fine. It's not a secret." Ben took a swig of his beer, then set the bottle down on the coffee table in front of the couch. He turned his whole body to face me, put his hands in his lap and took a deep breath. "In high school, I ran with a pretty rough crowd," he started.

"*You?*" I interrupted. He seemed so...clean cut.

"Yeah. My dad took off when I was a baby, and my mom worked two jobs to put food on the table, so she wasn't around much. I guess I was acting out. Anyway, Mrs. Valencia's daughter, Teresa, was part of that group."

"I had no idea Mrs. Valencia has a daughter," I said, surprised.

"*Had*." Ben stopped short. He took another deep breath before continuing.

"We were all out at the Rio Grande Gorge one weekend, just messing around, drinking some terrible strawberry wine that Kevin found in the back of his mom's liquor cabinet. We found a spot where the gorge dropped off sharply into the river, and we were daring each other to go to the edge and look down. It was stupid kid fun...until Kevin took things too far. He dared me, Teresa and another kid to climb down...threatened to make us walk home if we didn't." Ben swallowed hard. "We'd polished off the wine by that point and we were pretty good and buzzed. Teresa was always a daredevil anyway. She put us guys to shame." He smiled at a memory I could only imagine. "She went first. She sat on the edge of the drop off, scooted out and turned around to hang off the lip of that deep ravine. She held on for all of five seconds before the rocks she was holding onto crumbled."

I clamped my hand over my mouth. "What did you do?" I asked in a whisper.

"I tried to go down after her. Everyone else got in the car and took off. Kevin said they were going to get help. He lied. I made it a few feet down before I got stuck. It was hours before a hiker walked by and heard me calling out."

"Ben, I'm so sorry."

He gave me a weak smile. "It's in the past. And it's why I became a state police officer. Mrs. Valencia was devastated by the death of her daughter. And I got in a lot of trouble for being part of it. I was on the road to dropping out of school and doing God knows what with my life...but Mrs. Valencia forgave me, and she gave me a future. A future that maybe I didn't deserve. She tutored me so I could graduate on time, and she wrote the letter of recommendation that got me into the Academy."

"Wow," I said. The more I learned about my dear departed landlord, the more fascinated I was by her.

Someone knocked on the door. For an instant I thought it might be Tom, come to tell me I'd better be packing, and my heart skipped a beat. Then I remembered the pizza.

Ben answered the door and took the pizza to the kitchen table where we divvied it up. He wasn't joking about the green chile—it was slathered on half of the pepperoni pizza. "Let's watch a movie while we eat," I suggested, using my elbow to point toward the living room.

I moved over to the couch, plopped down, took a bite of the pizza—and immediately grabbed for my drink. "Oh my..." I started, then took another swig. "This is really hot!"

Ben stood doubled over between the couch and the kitchen, laughing so hard his pizza was starting to slide off his plate.

I tried to glare at him through the tears gushing from my eyes, but it only made him laugh harder. "Very funny!" I said, almost wheezing.

It took a minute for him to get a hold of himself, but Ben eventually responded. "It takes some getting used to. I promise it's a local favorite, though. No joke."

He went back to the kitchen, grabbed another slice of pizza, and brought it to my plate.

I bit into the slice of regular pepperoni pizza and moaned, "Oh, now *that's* good." I was so famished, I could eat the plate.

Ben found a cheesy old horror movie and we watched it in silence while we ate. Two pieces of chile-free pizza, one beer, and a swamp monster with a bad makeup job were the last things I remember before waking up Monday morning with my head on Ben's chest and a wicked ache in my back.

# CHAPTER THIRTEEN

---

I dropped Ben off at his apartment southwest of downtown around 9 a.m. and hit the coffee shop drive-through on my way back home. I debated going straight to Bianca's boutique to tell her about last night, but thought better of it when I reached out the window to take my coffee from the barista and got a whiff of myself. *Shower first.*

Not too much later, I was back on the road, headed toward downtown. Sitting at a stoplight, I stared at my hands on the steering wheel. Just a few months ago, I had a weekly manicure routine in Chicago that felt so important to me. I joked with Alex that I was going to my "therapy appointment" each Thursday during my lunch hour. It was an hour just for me, just for pampering. No clients demanding design changes. No employees missing deadlines. No arguing over who was making dinner that night. It was an hour where I could just...relax.

The universe must have heard my thoughts, because the moment I turned down the next street, I saw a sign. Literally. The beautifully decorated chalkboard sign outside the pristine façade of an Italianate style building was too far away to read more than one word—but it was the only word I needed to see to immediately turn right and into the parking lot of the retail park.

*Salon!* Relaxing for an hour or so while getting my ragged nails properly trimmed and polished was just what the doctor ordered this morning. I hadn't realized how badly I needed some space and time to clear my head. I prayed the nail technician wasn't a talker.

I pulled open the glass door of the swanky salon, and instead of the tinkle of bells I expected to hear, an electronic motion sensor sang a little tune as I walked in.

"Welcome to Rio Blanco Salon and Spa! How may I help you?" A perky young blond woman sat at the glass reception desk, a genuine smile stretching over her red-lipped mouth.

"I need a manicure. Is someone available?" I asked, wiggling my nails in her direction.

"Absolutely! Have a seat and Corey will be right with you," she responded.

I took a seat on a plush white loveseat as the receptionist ducked around the corner into the salon. Bronze statues of coyotes, foxes and birds dotted the low glass tables between neat piles of the latest fashion magazines. I looked down at my brown leather booties sinking into the thick, cream and caramel-colored carpet. This place was *posh*. This manicure was going to cost a fortune.

I grabbed my cell phone and checked my bank account balance. *Looks like I'm going to be eating ramen for the next week.* I thought about sneaking out while the receptionist was gone, and then I heard a woman's voice—slightly familiar—spilling down the hall. "...acted like I was out of my mind. I just needed some information!"

Another voice—soft but distinctly male—followed, "Honey, the ink was still wet on the old bat's death certificate. You know I adore you, but you jump the gun sometimes."

The woman sighed loudly enough that I could hear it all the way in the reception area. "I've just been waiting for this for so long. It's the last piece I need."

The perky receptionist rounded the corner and beamed another white-toothed smile in my direction. "Corey's ready for you. She's asked me to bring you back."

I returned the smile and stood to follow. As we walked around the wall behind the reception desk and entered the salon area, my suspicions were confirmed. Birdie Lemon was sitting in a chair with her blond hair in foils.

The man standing behind Birdie, putting in the last of the foils, was tall and slightly paunchy around the middle. He wore black from head to toe, punctuated only by the frosted tips of his hair. He looked up at me as I passed and gave me a friendly smile and nod.

In the mirror, I saw the slightest frown cross Birdie's face, but she replaced it instantly with a placid smile when she saw me looking.

"This way!" the receptionist said, leading me to the other side of the room where two tables sat side-by-side. "This is Corey," she said. "She'll take good care of you. Have fun!" With that, she turned and left.

Sitting behind the table on the left was a young woman with black hair slicked up and back in a six-inch mohawk. She gave me a curt smile and asked, "What are we doing today?"

As I sat in the well-padded red leather seat across the table from her, I answered, "French manicure, please."

Her eyebrows rose. "Don't do many of those these days," she said as she took my hands and looked over my nails. She flipped my hands over and looked at my palms. "Artist?"

I nodded.

Her eyes flicked up to examine my face. "You're not an artist," she said simply.

I pulled my hands back and placed them on my lap. "Excuse me?"

"Your hands aren't rough enough for a sculptor or jewelry artist. You don't have paint under your nails, so you can't be a painter. Your hair needs a bit of a trim, but it's not a total disaster. And you're *here*. We don't get many artists here." Corey sat back in her chair and watched my face.

I schooled my expression the best I could, but

inside I felt furious. How *dare* this total stranger presume to know anything about me.

*Two can play at this game.*

"You're right. I'm not making a living as an artist yet—I just left my job and moved here to give it a go," I said. "So maybe it's a leap to say I'm an artist. But at least I'm not a bored trust-fund baby." I crossed my arms and glared at the woman. Corey couldn't have been more than 25, and she had that look of entitlement and snobbery I'd seen all too often in the new hires at the creative agency.

I was surprised when her expression changed from a smirk to an authentic smile. She leaned forward again, rested her elbows on the table and folded her hands under her chin. "French manicure, huh?" She pushed two small bowls of water toward me from the edge of the table. "Soak 'em."

I didn't move.

"I like you," she said at my hesitation. "You're a people watcher, like me. I can tell."

"I like to think I'm just detail-oriented," I said, slowly uncrossing my arms.

I heard Birdie talking across the room, at a lower

volume this time. "Do you have everything for the event?" she said in a near whisper.

I kept my ears tuned to Birdie's conversation, but the rest she said so quietly I couldn't make any sense of it.

"What's up with you and Birdie?" Corey asked, raising her eyebrows in Birdie's direction.

I slid my fingertips into the water and shrugged. "I don't know what you're talking about."

"I saw the way she looked at you when you walked by. And you're clearly eavesdropping."

"How did she look at me?" I asked, pointedly ignoring the eavesdropping comment.

"It's okay. You don't have to pretend. Most women in this town don't get along with Birdie. She's either after something you have, or you're after something *she* has." Corey pulled my right hand out of the water and began cutting my nails into neat round shapes.

"You grew up in Santa Fe, didn't you," I stated. I wasn't sure I liked this woman yet, but I was curious about her—and more curious about what she knew.

She smiled but didn't meet my eyes. "As you

said. Trust-fund baby. My family is pretty entrenched here."

I turned around to make sure Birdie was far enough away that couldn't hear us talking. "What do you know about Birdie's interest in the Valencia property?" I asked.

"Last I heard, it was the only house on that block that she didn't have a contract on. She wants to build some new-age wellness center. After her last project flopped so badly, she's probably trying to redeem herself." Corey grinned. "Maybe I'll move my business there. Better part of downtown, more interesting people to watch."

"What happened with her last project?" I prodded.

"She greased a lot of palms to get a luxury condo project approved for out near the Opera. A couple days after they broke ground, they found relics."

"Relics?

"Yup. Tesuque relics." Corey filed my nails as she talked. "Birdie says they were planted. The historic foundation disagreed. Project was shut down, and Birdie was out a bunch of money." She whispered conspiratorially. "And some of it wasn't hers. So I hear."

Just then, Birdie walked by in a cloud of expensive perfume, headed for what looked like the restroom at the back of the salon.

"I'll be right back," I said, pulling my hand out of Corey's grip. "Need to use the restroom."

She raised one eyebrow at me but said nothing.

I followed the smell of perfume to the door marked "women" and turned the handle. The door was locked.

It was at least five minutes before Birdie emerged. I had half a mind to ask what she was doing in there, but I controlled myself.

She stopped short when she saw me standing outside the door.

"Hi," I said. "Remember me?"

Birdie frowned, her full, pink lips beautiful even then. "You're the artist living in the Little House at Villa Valencia."

"You asked me to reach out to you if I learned anything about what Tom is going to do with the property. I've been meaning to call, but you know, settling into a new city and all," I droned, looking casually at my clean-cut but still-unpolished nails. "It's convenient running into you here." I looked around as if I were checking for eavesdroppers. "I might have some information for you."

Birdie put her hand on my arm and guided me further down the hall, away from the salon. She whispered, "What do you know?"

"First...what's in it for me?" I asked.

"What do you mean?" Birdie crossed her thin arms and drew herself up taller.

"I mean that Mrs. Valencia let me rent the Little House for a song. I hear you want to tear it down and build a spa."

"A health center," she corrected me.

I wasn't completely sure this conversation was going to get me the information I needed from Birdie, but I had to try something. There were more suspects in this murder than I could shake a stick at, and I was running out of time.

"Is that what you argued about the night she was murdered?" I asked.

Birdie's arms dropped to her side and she ground her jaw. "You're fishing," she said. "I should have known. Any friend of Rocky's..."

"So what did you argue about, then?" I pushed her.

"I didn't argue about *anything* with that woman

that night. I was out to dinner with my husband. In fact, I hadn't seen her since the last SFPAA meeting."

"Where did you go to dinner?" I asked.

"I'm not answering any more of your questions. You're not a cop and I'm not a suspect." Birdie lifted her chin and looked down her too-perfect-to-be-natural nose at me.

I shrugged. "Okay." I turned on my heel and went back to the table where Corey was waiting for me, her hand over her mouth stifling her laughter. As tempted as I was to see Birdie's reaction, I stopped myself from turning back and looking at her.

"That was the most entertaining thing I've seen all week," Corey said, grabbing one of my hands and beginning to paint white tips on my nails. Her shoulders shook with barely contained giggles.

"You heard all that, huh?" I looked around the room, wondering who else might have overheard the conversation. "I wanted to get Birdie's alibi for the night my landlord was murdered," I admitted. "She doesn't seem to be the most...honest person. I thought maybe riling her up would get her to reveal more. I think it worked."

"Now things are getting *really* interesting. I've got a regular armchair detective here at my table."

I made a face at Corey. Out of the corner of my eye, I saw Birdie walk by—as far away from me as she could get in the small salon—and plop down into the stylist's chair. She whispered animatedly, her manicured hand waving around like she was swatting a fly. The stylist nodded along, every once in a while looking over at me.

It was starting to make me paranoid.

"If anyone was going to argue with Mrs. Valencia that night, it would be him," Corey said, nodding her head toward the stylist. "But he was here late doing an emergency color fix for the mayor's daughter—she was getting married the next day, and Stan is the go-to stylist in town for event prep. The salon looked like a war zone Saturday morning."

"Who is that?" I asked, indicating with my eyes that I was talking about the stylist. "And why would he argue with Mrs. Valencia?"

"That's Stan Lieberman. Mrs. Valencia cost him a lot of business over the last month," she answered.

"*That's* Stan?"

"You've heard of him?"

"My friend Bianca told me a little bit about that situation," I shared.

"Bianca Romero?" Corey asked, stopping her work to stare at me.

"Yes..." I said, suspicious.

She smiled. "I knew I liked you. It never ceases to amaze me just how small this town is. Bianca is good people. Her boutique is one of the few in town that sells genuine local handiwork—not that cheap, made-in-China crap. My brother started his business selling his hand-painted, beaded leather jackets there."

I relaxed my shoulders, relieved. "Bianca really believes in the community here. It's one of the reasons I moved here," I said, looking at Corey's handiwork on my fingertips.

"Where did you move here from?"

"Chicago."

"Long way."

"Not long enough." I gave Corey a pinched smile. "But there's something special about Santa Fe. When Bianca moved here after college, I visited when I could. It never felt like I was here long enough. I always craved more."

Corey's eyes darkened. "It's a special place, all right. But it's not what it used to be. A lot of money has moved in—with people like her." Corey jerked her thumb toward Birdie, not even looking to see if she was watching. "The culture is dying. Some of us want to fix that." She leaned down and pulled something out of a drawer. When she held it out to me, I could see that it was a business card.

I took the card from her. It had a single word on the front: *SAM*. I turned it over in my hand and saw that a matching website URL was the only thing on the back. I raised my eyebrows in Corey's direction.

"Southwest Art Mutiny," she said with a mischievous grin. "When you're tired of playing by the rules of the elite, check us out. We'll get you connected to the *real* art scene in Santa Fe." Corey winked at me.

I smiled. *What a weird woman. What a weird place. I love it here.*

After paying for my manicure, I sat in my Jeep for a few minutes staring at that card. I wondered what SAM was about. I also hesitated to get too involved in the community—any community—here knowing I might not be able to stay. My heart ached.

I'd dawdled long enough. It was time to go see my best friend and fill her in on last night's events before she found me and throttled me. I started the car and headed to the Desert Wind Boutique.

# CHAPTER FOURTEEN

---

The little brass bells on the door tinkled cheerfully when I walked in. Bianca was behind the register, handing a young couple their purchases. She waved me over.

"You've got a lot of nerve," she said, crossing her arms across her ample bosom.

"I apologized to Ben..." I started.

Bianca cut me off. "You've got a lot of nerve going to talk to Tom and Kathy without me, then not even calling me and telling me about it. I had to hear about everything secondhand from Rocky!"

I couldn't tell how much of this was genuine anger, and how much was a show. Bianca could be a bit of a drama queen sometimes. In college she directed that energy to acting onstage at the annual Shakespeare Festival in Boulder. Since then she's put her flair for drama into her window displays at the boutique—but sometimes I got the sense that decorating a window wasn't enough for her, and the need to put on a show just *leaked out*.

"I'm sorry," I said. Apologizing seemed like a safe bet no matter whether her fury was real or a show. "I've got more to fill you in on than Rocky even knows," I said, whispering behind my hand as if someone were listening. "Can you take a break?"

Bianca's face softened and she smiled impishly. "Serena! I'm going out," she called out.

Desert Wind's newest employee weaved her way through racks of clothing and emerged behind the front counter. "I got it, boss," the redhead said with a mock salute. Serena was tall, bony and speckled with freckles. She stuck out like a poppy in the sagebrush.

"Nancy's in the back doing inventory, so holler at her if you need any help. I'll be back in a bit," Bianca said to Serena.

As I walked by the jewelry display case that served as the front counter, I noticed a collection of silver charms. One of them was shaped like a tiny hammer. It brought to mind the hammer that David was wielding in Felicia's gallery yesterday.

"I need to stop by Phil's Hardware while we're out," I commented.

"Fine by me. I need more yard lights," Bianca said as we walked through the shop door and out into the midday sun.

"No, you really don't. You're going to blind your neighbors," I joked.

Bianca scowled at me.

Two blocks off the plaza, the boutique was in the middle of a strip of other shops, with houses-turned-galleries across the street. We made our way to where the Jeep was parked in the underground parking garage near the library.

Even 30 feet from my Jeep and in the dim light of the parking garage, I knew something was wrong.

I ran up and stopped short, Bianca hot on my heels. "Sonofa..." I hissed when I saw the destruction. Several deep gouges ran horizontally from the front panel of the Jeep to the back bumper on the driver's side.

Bianca gasped. "It looks like someone keyed your car...with a broadsword."

I ran my hands along one of the gashes. "Or the claw of a hammer," I said.

"You don't think..."

"That's exactly what I think. Someone doesn't want me getting involved. And clearly I'm onto something if they're bold enough to do something like this in broad daylight."

"I'll call Rocky. You'll need to report this, and maybe he can get the security camera footage." Bianca dialed her phone and paced as she filled in her husband on what had happened. "He'll be here soon," she told me after she hung up. Bianca put her arm around my shoulders. "I'm sorry about your Jeep."

I tried to laugh, but it came out like a grunt. "This town has not been kind to my poor old Jeep. First it was doused in red paint, then Ben scratched it with his gun belt, now this." I patted the blue hood. "Poor ol' girl. You deserve better. We'll get you patched up and you'll be good as new."

I turned to Bianca. "I think this means I'm getting close. Too close for the murderer's comfort."

"Fill me in on what you know so far," Bianca

prompted. She leaned on the driver's side door and crossed her arms.

"I know that Mrs. Valencia was bludgeoned to death with a hammer in her home next to a very famous and very pricey painting—which, other than some blood splatter, was untouched. I know a lot of people hated her, or at least had motive to kill her, but so far everyone has an alibi.

"Tom didn't have a great relationship with his mother, and he's going to benefit from the inheritance, but I don't think he wanted to hurt her. He was in Albuquerque at the time of the murder anyway.

"Kathy seems nuts enough to do it, and she was angry at Mrs. Valencia for kicking her out of the Little House—but she was busy stalking Ben at your party when the murder happened.

"Birdie wants the land that Villa Valencia sits on—but she was out to dinner with her husband. Stan is angry that Mrs. Valencia badmouthed him and cost him business, but he was working late at the salon that night.

"Aaron wanted Mrs. Valencia to part with her Navarro painting—a private collector offered him a fortune to get it for him—and Mrs. Valencia wouldn't budge. But Aaron was seen on camera hanging a collection of paintings at a gallery across town.

"That leaves David Ramirez, the contractor that Mrs. Valencia owed money to. I ran into him at Felicia's gallery yesterday. He was hammering nails into the wall, helping Aaron hang a large painting. The hammer looked an awful lot like the one that killed Mrs. Valencia. But Ben said David's alibi checked out, that he was checking on a remodeling job out near the closed-down university."

Rocky pulled up in his Charger. "You know, it would be nice to see you *without* a crime having been committed for a change," he joked as he got out of the car.

"Cute," I said.

Rocky walked around my Jeep. "Ouch. That's gonna be a heck of a job for a body shop." He bent down to look closer at the gouges. "We get a lot of reports of keyed cars downtown, but whatever did this was definitely bigger than a key."

"I think it looks like the claw of a hammer," I said, crossing my arms. "Don't you?"

"Yeah, that could've done it." Rocky stood up and frowned. "Ali, I don't like this. This was a warning. You really need to let us handle this. Let the violent crimes unit do the investigating and ask the questions."

"You guys aren't acting fast enough," I argued. "The murderer could be long gone by the time you figure them out." *And I'll be out on the street.*

"We have procedures in place for a reason. 'Innocent until proven guilty'—it's the foundation of our legal system. It takes time to process the evidence, question suspects, follow up on alibis..."

"Meanwhile the murderer is threatening an innocent woman," I said, crossing my arms.

Rocky sighed and looked at the dingy ceiling of the parking garage. His eyes passed over his wife's face before landing back on mine. "You're not just putting yourself in danger, here. Bianca could get hurt, too." He swallowed. "And I would never forgive you for that."

I felt the blood drain from my face.

"We'll be careful," Bianca almost whispered. "We're smart women, you know."

"You're smart, *period*," Rocky agreed. "But I love you, Bianca. And Ali, I can put up with you." His smile didn't reach his eyes. "Butt out. Both of you."

After Rocky got what he needed from us to make the report, Bianca and I took my poor shredded Jeep over to Phil's Hardware Store.

"You still want to help me with this. Even with Rocky warning us off?" I asked her as we drove.

"Yes. Absolutely," she said. I kept my eyes on the road, but I could hear the determination in her voice.

I got her caught up on everything that had happened. Bianca nodded ruefully when I told her what Ben had shared about Teresa's death. "I know the story," she said. "It's certainly a 'beauty from ashes' situation. It could have ruined Ben's life—but instead he turned himself around and became an incredible man and an outstanding officer."

"It sounded to me like a lot of that was thanks to Mrs. Valencia," I said, pulling the Jeep into a parking spot right near the front door of the small hardware store. I turned off the engine and turned to Bianca. "*She* could have ruined his life for that. Instead she forgave him and even helped him get into the Academy."

The corners of Bianca's lightly glossed lips turned down. "She was a powerhouse of a woman. She could be so...stubborn. Righteous. Feisty." She shook her head. "But she had some good in her too. This world has lost a very interesting human being."

"Let's see if we can figure out why." I opened the door and got out of the car. The blazing hot desert sun on the top of my head felt like a giant was frying me under a magnifying glass.

Brass bells clanged when I pushed open the door of the hardware store and held it for Bianca to follow me through. I couldn't see anyone behind the counter, but there were a few other patrons milling about between the low shelves.

"Bianca!" a voice said from the back of the shop. A tall man with snow-white hair and an overly tanned face walked out from a door to our left, behind a long counter that ran almost the entire length of the shop. He flipped up a section of the counter and walked around to throw his arms around Bianca. She was a good foot shorter than him, but she returned his embrace with equal enthusiasm.

"How is Linette?" Bianca asked him when he finally released her. "She done with chemo now?"

"Her last appointment was two weeks ago," he answered. "She'll be thrilled that I saw you today. She's still raving about those lemon bars."

Bianca beamed. "Tell her I'll come by soon with a fresh batch."

The man's sobered. "Thank you. We're not out of the woods yet. The doctors are monitoring her closely—we're praying there's no recurrence."

Bianca took both of his hands in his. "Rocky and I will keep praying for her. And for you."

The man nodded, his lips pinched but smiling.

"Phil, this is Ali," Bianca said, releasing his hands and nodding her head toward me. "She just moved into the Little House at Villa Valencia. I was hoping you could help her with something."

"Oh my! Lots happening at the Valencia property over the last week. Poor Mrs. Valencia. Poor Tom." Phil shook his head sadly. "Such tragedy in that family." He looked me up and down, worrying at his chin with his index finger. "I remember you."

I nodded. "I was in here last week for paint cleaning supplies."

"Ah, yes! I never forget a face." Phil smiled from ear to ear.

"I'm doing my part to try to help figure out who killed Mrs. Valencia," I volunteered. "I got a good look at the hammer that was used, and I was hoping to take a look at your selection here to see if any of the brands looked familiar." I kept quiet about the hammer David Ramirez had been using at the gallery—no need to cast any suspicion unnecessarily at this point.

"Of course," Phil said, waving for us to follow. He took us almost all the way to the back of the store to an aisle with hand tools. He pointed to a selection of hammers.

I thanked him and leaned down to take a closer look.

"I'll be up at the register if you need me," he said. "Bianca, it was so great to see you." With that, he disappeared back into the maze of aisles.

I counted six different brands of hammers—and they all looked identical. Identical to each other, identical to the hammer I saw at the house, and identical to the hammer I saw David wielding at the gallery. The only difference was the color—three were blue and three were red. I swore under my breath.

"This is a dead end," I said to Bianca.

She tucked a long lock of black hair behind her ear. "I'm sorry. I was hoping this would help."

I sighed. "It did help. At least now I can stop obsessing over David. He has an alibi, and the hammer I saw him with—which looked like the one at the murder scene—looks like every other hammer here." I put my hands on my hips. "I've hit a wall. It's time to get creative."

# CHAPTER FIFTEEN

---

I tossed and turned all that night, and woke up Tuesday morning feeling like I'd been run over by a train. I chugged some coffee, grabbed a cheese stick out of the fridge, then packed up my plein air painting supplies and headed to the plaza.

For me, the act of creating was not only meditative, it could be stimulating too. It used my brain in a different way and opened up new channels of thinking. When I was faced with an internal challenge or I needed to make a difficult decision, painting or drawing could stir new ideas and answers. Painting also gave me a sense of control when things felt *out* of control—and loosened me up when I was feeling tightly wound.

For me, it was a balm that soothed almost any trouble.

Hitting a wall in the Valencia case left me craving a paintbrush in my hand. To figure out my next step, I knew I needed to stop thinking and start intuiting. There was no better way for me to switch gears than to put paint to canvas.

The plaza was busy that morning, and I had to park a few blocks away. I was grateful for the nylon carryall and portable easel I had splurged on early that summer when I was still in Chicago. I had had high hopes of painting people and scenes on the Magnificent Mile, and honing my skills for capturing movement. Painting portraits and still-life scenes had always come rather naturally to me. The challenge was capturing life as it happened.

I never got the chance to paint on the Magnificent Mile. The one and only time I had brought these plein air painting supplies out and used them was on the balcony of the hotel room I had rented briefly when I moved out of the apartment I shared with Alex.

Walking through downtown Santa Fe with my gear slung across my back, I remembered that day. I had felt like my heart was in a million pieces, and maybe creating a bit of beauty would somehow start gluing the pieces back together. I bought a bouquet of flowers from the florist down the street, then set up a still-life scene out on the glass table on the hotel balcony.

As I pushed the paint around the first canvas, something unexpected emerged. The flowers were unlike anything else I had ever painted. They were bold, with imprecise lines and daring brushstrokes. The scene practically jumped off the canvas.

I set the first painting aside to dry and loaded the easel with a second blank canvas. Once again, when my brush hit the surface, something came over me. The still-life came to life under my hands. Painting those flowers was almost an out-of-body experience.

By the end of the day, I had completed three flower paintings—and I didn't know what to think of them. They had captured something of my heart that had never seen the light of day, and I wasn't sure I wanted to show them to anyone.

Now in Santa Fe, I wondered what Felicia might think of them. She said I had an eye...but I wondered what she would think about a painting that came from my heart instead of my artist's eye.

I felt my spirit lift just a little bit. Maybe, if I could find a way to stay in this town, I would muster up the courage to show her those works.

I made it to the square in the center of the plaza and found an empty park bench facing the jewelry artists that lined up along the Palace of the Governors. It was always a sight to behold. Dozens of Native American artists sat along the wall that ran the length of the north side of the square, their blankets splayed in front of them, and their beautiful handmade jewelry laid out lovingly on those blankets.

Even from across the street I could see the glint of silver on many of those blankets. I itched to walk over and touch the delicate works of wearable art—but I was there for a purpose and I needed to stay focused.

It took me just a few minutes to get the easel set up and my paint ready on my small palette. It took me longer to choose a subject. There were so many beautiful faces there that morning, so many stories I wanted to capture on my canvas.

I finally decided on a family toward the eastern end of the row of blankets. A woman with two children—a little girl who looked to be about five years old, and an older boy of maybe 10—caught my attention with their smiles. They had the warmest, most welcoming smiles. Nearly every shopper that walked along the line of vendors stopped in front of that family, no doubt because of those delightfully friendly faces. I was sure the jewelry was beautiful too, but those smiles shone brighter than any silver.

As I painted the first rough layer, getting the proportions and angles down properly, I thought about all that had happened in the last few days. The conversation with Aaron at Felicia's gallery bubbled to the surface of my mind, and I remembered something he had said about *no one refuses the Valencias, it doesn't end well*. It implied something sinister. It made me think of the stories of organized crime back in Chicago. I wondered if Mrs. Valencia was mixed up with the mob.

I laughed at myself. This was Santa Fe. Not Chicago or New York, or even San Francisco. Still, though, the more I learned about my deceased landlord, the more intriguing and complex the woman became. She was more than met the eye.

Birdie was more than met the eye, too. The woman clearly had a lot of sway in this town, and she exerted it openly. She's another woman who likely wouldn't be denied. I wondered if her clash with Mrs. Valencia caused more of an explosion than anyone realized.

The world around me came back into focus when I noticed people were starting to gather around me in the square. I did my best to ignore the audience—painting in front of people was also something I wanted to get more skilled at—but it was hard.

It took me about two hours to get to a point with the painting where I felt like I would ruin it if I kept working on it. The smiling faces of the Native American family beamed at me from two places, now: the canvas on my easel and the Palace of the Governors across the street. The crowd around me had never dispersed, only grown.

While I was able to lose myself in the process of painting, there was something about having an audience that stopped my mind from working on the problem of who killed Mrs. Valencia. As I packed up my supplies and got ready to head back home, I knew I was no closer to solving the crime.

# CHAPTER SIXTEEN

———

I went home to the Little House feeling discouraged. I felt like I was missing something right in front of my nose.

I pulled out the drawings I did the night of the murder and scoured them for clues. Nothing was triggering any useful insight. *Maybe my subconscious will work on it if I just distract myself for a while. Even Sherlock Holmes played the violin to give his subconscious a chance to work on a problem.*

I was in my living room putting boxes together around 11 a.m. when my phone rang. I didn't recognize the number, so I let it go to voicemail. When I listened to the message a moment later, I didn't know if I should laugh or cringe. So I did both.

"Ms. Porter, this is Trevor, Lawrence Lemon's assistant. That's Lawrence Lemon of Lemon, Trinidad and Associates." The man's voice was nasal, on the verge of whiny—and yet at the same time, robotic. "He had expected you to call by now. He needs a portrait for the office redesign by the end of August. Please call me back so we can get the project set up."

*So many assumptions in such a short message. And where did he get my number, anyway?*

I was just about to call him back when I heard a knock at the door. My heart skipped, hoping it was Ben.

It was not Ben.

Peering back at me through the small window in the door was Aaron Taylor. I opened the door about a foot, enough to casually lean on the frame and block any view he had into my home.

Aaron stood on my front step, looking down his nose at me, per usual.

"What do you want?" I asked the haughty art dealer.

"I'm looking for David. Have you seen him?"

"No. Why don't you call him?"

Aaron rolled his eyes. "Why do you think I'm *here?*" He waved a long-fingered hand at the main house. "He hasn't been answering his phone or returning my messages. He didn't show up to put together the second display for me last night. This is totally unlike the man."

"Still doesn't explain why you're here." I cocked an eyebrow at him.

Aaron stepped back and stood near the bistro table on my patio. I didn't move from my position in the doorway. "The last thing David said was that he had a job to collect on. The Valencia project was the only one I know of that he wasn't paid for recently. No one is answering the door at the main house. And since you're an unemployed artist, I knew you'd be home, so I figured I'd ask you if you'd seen him." He looked at me as though he were waiting for a reaction.

I didn't give him one.

I looked at him impassively, racking my brain for something I could say to end the conversation.

Aaron turned back to face me, cocked his head to the side as if he were studying me, then spun on his heel and faced the main house. "I'm not greedy, you know," he said without looking at me.

"I never said you were," I responded, wondering where he was going with this.

"I can tell that you think I have...ulterior motives. But I have a reputation to uphold. I moved here a couple of years ago from New York, and my clientele pay me top dollar because I can always find exactly what they're looking for."

"Your client must have been really upset when the Camino became evidence in a murder investigation," I pointed out.

"The painting is still in there," Aaron said, pointing to the main house. "I saw it through the front window. The police didn't take it. It has just a little bit of blood splatter on it. Nothing I can't clean with a careful application of turpentine."

"So why aren't you making a play for it?" I asked.

"You really do think I'm a lowlife." Aaron turned to face me again.

I was surprised to see that he didn't look hurt or angry—just curious.

"Mrs. Valencia and I had our differences," he continued, "but I respected her. I'll respect her memory, too. Tom can keep that painting."

I heard my phone ringing in the living room and turned toward the sound. I nodded at Aaron and said, "I have to get that. I'll tell David you were looking for him if I see him around."

Aaron nodded back, then left through the side yard of the main house.

The phone had gone to voicemail by the time I got to it, and there was a text message from Rocky: CALL ME BACK. So I did.

He picked up after one ring and didn't even say hello. "Kathy's gone."

"What?" I said. I slid down to the couch, my heart racing.

"We're not even sure how it's possible." Rocky was talking fast. "She had two cracked ribs, a broken collarbone and a concussion. She shouldn't even be awake, much less up and walking. But she walked right out of St. Vincent's, slipped right past the staff."

"Any idea where she went?" I asked, horrified.

"No. But I want you and Ben to be on the lookout. It wouldn't surprise me if she made a beeline toward one of you."

I swallowed hard, then got up and locked my

door. "Okay. Have you talked to Ben about this yet?"

"I tried," Rocky said. "He didn't answer his phone. If you talk to him before I do, warn him."

"I will."

After I hung up with Rocky, I sat for a moment at the kitchen table in stunned silence. It took a few minutes to get my wits about me. This woman had a track record of bizarre behavior, she was angry with me for whatever reason, and I was still not totally convinced that she didn't have something to do with Mrs. Valencia's murder. Suddenly I felt very, very alone in that house. *When I'm finally settled in a place, I need to get a big, mean dog.*

I picked up my phone and called Ben. No answer. I tried to remember what he had told me about his week—I wasn't paying much attention to his words. I was lost in thought driving him home yesterday morning, replaying the night before and trying to sort out how I felt about it. I seemed to remember he said his next shift didn't start until later in the day. It was approaching lunchtime now—maybe he was in the shower getting ready for work.

I started for the door, thinking I'd drive over to

Ben's apartment and bang on the door—and my phone rang again. *What the heck? I never get this many calls in one day!*

I didn't recognize the number, but I went ahead and answered, just in case.

"Alissandra? This is Trevor again. Lawrence Lemon's assistant. Did I catch you at a good time?"

*Wow, this guy is aggressive.* "Not really. I'm on my way out the door right now. And call me Ali."

"Then I'll keep this brief, Ali. When can you start the portrait?"

"Whoa whoa whoa," I said, stopping where I stood. "We have a lot to discuss before I can get Mr. Lemon scheduled. We need to talk about the size of the canvas, the color palette, the background he wants, his clothing choices...and once I have all that information, I need to give him a timeline and quote." I was already feeling frustrated by Lawrence's assistant. Working with the man himself was probably going to be a nightmare. But I really needed the money.

"Come by tomorrow and he'll answer any questions you have. And he's happy to pay a rush fee if you can get this done in three weeks," Trevor said.

"Three weeks? That's not possible," I said, my head spinning.

"Make it possible. After all, the faster you do the job, the faster you get paid."

"But you don't even know what my going rate is."

"Mr. Lemon has lived in Santa Fe his entire life. He knows art. He knows how artists work. I'm sure your rate is fine. He just needs this done so his wife will...be free to move on to other projects."

*Birdie.* Suddenly Lawrence's insistence made much more sense.

"Fine," I said, defeated. "I'll be by at 10 tomorrow morning."

I was already regretting this project when I hung up the phone.

§

I pounded on the door to Ben's apartment and shouted his name. No answer.

After a few more attempts at increasing volume, a man poked his head out of another apartment door down the hall. "He's not there," said the plump, balding man. "I saw him leave an hour ago."

"Thanks," I said. "Any idea where he went?"

The man turned up his nose at me. "I'm not his keeper," he said before he slammed the door so loud it echoed down the hall.

*It's just not my day for getting along with people.* I pulled out my phone and tried to call Ben again.

I heard the phone ringing inside his apartment.

"Not good," I whispered to no one. What if he was hurt? What if Kathy was in there murdering him?

I jiggled the door handle. Locked.

I went around the back side of the long, one-story apartment building and approached the iron fence that cordoned off Ben's tiny backyard. At least I *thought* it was his backyard. It was hard to tell on the other side of the building.

I planted my foot on the bar at the bottom of the fence and was about to try to hoist myself up over the top of the six-foot bars when I heard someone call my name.

I turned toward the sound and saw Ben running up to me—decked out in shorts, running shoes and a sweat-soaked t-shirt.

"What are you doing?" he asked as he skidded

to a stop next to me. "Breaking and entering is a crime, you know."

I jumped down and threw my arms around him. "You stink," I said, pulling away after a good, long embrace. I ducked my head, hoping my face wouldn't reveal the relief flooding me and threatening to make me cry.

"Well, I've been running in this heat, so...duh. Why are you climbing my fence?"

"You weren't answering your phone. Then you weren't answering your door. And I heard your phone ringing inside...so I thought..."

Ben's face darkened. "That's kind of scary behavior, Ali. I don't answer my phone and you try to break into my house? Not okay."

I immediately realized the path his mind must be going down. "No! No. I'm not stalking you. It's not like that..."

"Then what's it like?" He took a step back and crossed his arms.

I crossed my arms too, now feeling defensive. "Kathy left the hospital. No one knows where she is. I was worried she might hurt you. Clearly there's nothing to worry about. Have a good day." I pushed past Ben and started walking back around the building to my scarred Jeep.

Ben grabbed my arm. I stopped and spun. "Let go of me."

He put his hands up. "I'm sorry," he said. "I'm a little gun-shy after Kathy."

I put my hands on my hips and looked at him, not saying a word.

"Really, I'm sorry. I shouldn't have even thought that about you."

"No, you shouldn't have." I retorted. "I'm a lot of things, but I'm not a stalker."

Ben looked past me. "What the heck?"

I turned to see that he was looking at the gouges in the side of my Jeep. "A little worse than the scratch *you* left, huh?" I said, nodding toward it.

Ben walked over to the vehicle and crouched down to see the damage. "Who did this?"

I shrugged. "Your guess is as good as mine."

He stood up and looked at me with much kinder eyes than he had just a few minutes ago. "Tell me what happened."

"I went to Bianca's boutique this morning and I parked in the underground lot by the library. When I came back to my car, it was like this."

"Were any other vehicles damaged?" Ben asked.

"No, Officer Goodson. No other vehicles were damaged." I smiled at him, appreciating the concern.

"This is no joke, Ali. This looks like a warning."

I scratched the back of my neck and looked down. "I was thinking the same thing."

"Maybe you should back off," Ben said, putting his hand on my shoulder. "Let the cops handle this."

"Look, I trust the cops here. I mean, they were smart enough to hire Rocky." I grinned weakly. "But finding out who murdered Mrs. Valencia is the only way Tom is going to let me stay in the Little House. And I can't afford to live anywhere else right now."

"I'm sure Rocky and Bianca would let you..."

I cut him off. "No. They've done enough for me. Besides, they don't have room—I'd be on the couch and in the way. And I couldn't paint there. I need to have space to paint if I'm going to make a living as an artist." I looked at my feet. "If I can't make it work here, I'm going to have to do the unthinkable."

"And what's that?" Ben pressed. He moved a step closer to me.

"Move in with my parents in California until I can find another agency job."

Silence hung in the air like a thick morning fog. Ben finally broke the silence. "I don't want you to leave."

"I don't want to leave either. And it might kill me to have to live with my parents—assuming they'd even *let* me stay. We're not on the best terms."

"Still, though, that's better than what could happen if you keep getting involved in the Valencia case," Ben said.

I tilted my head at him. "It almost sounds like *you* don't want me involved."

"It's just that..."

The sound of my phone ringing cut off whatever Ben was about to say. I looked at the screen to see it was Rocky calling and I answered immediately.

"We found Kathy," he said slowly.

"Oh, thank goodness," I said, heaving a sigh of relief. I repeated the news to Ben, who was watching me closely. "Where was she?"

"Her body was found in Footbridges Park."

# CHAPTER SEVENTEEN

---

I pulled the phone away from my ear and stared at it. This day just kept getting more bizarre. "Her...body?" I asked Rocky as I put the phone back to my ear.

"Looks like a suicide," he answered. "But it's suspicious enough, the investigators are looking into the possibility of foul play."

Ben was making hand gestures at me, clearly wanting to know what I was hearing. I held a finger up.

"How did she die?"

It took a moment for Rocky to answer, and when he did, it was in a hushed tone. "Looks like her head hit a rock."

I swallowed and looked back at Ben. His eyes were pleading.

"Can you come down to the park?" Rocky asked. "There's an object here I wonder if you can identify. Or maybe Ben can—I'm trying to get in touch with him, too."

"He's right here," I said.

Rocky chuckled. "Of course he is."

I glared at the phone. "We'll be right over."

When I hung up with Rocky, I gave Ben the recap. He didn't even bother changing his clothes—we got into his black Honda Civic and headed straight to the park.

§

I found it a bit surreal that I hadn't even been in Santa Fe for a week and I was at my second crime scene. I looked around the narrow park and saw a mix of uniforms and plainclothes ducking in and out of the taped-off area.

Ben and I stood under a cottonwood tree, both trying to spot Rocky in the hubbub.

"Over here!" Rocky yelled from somewhere behind us.

I spotted him waving, and nudged Ben to follow me. Rocky was standing near the edge of the dry riverbed. As we approached, I could see he was holding a clear plastic bag with what appeared to be a belt in it.

I leaned in to get a closer look at the belt. It looked familiar, but it took me a moment to place it. "That looks similar to the belt David Ramirez was wearing when I saw him at Southwest Treasures yesterday."

"The general contractor?" Rocky clarified.

"That's him," I confirmed. "Aaron came looking for him this morning. Said he didn't show up for a job and he isn't answering his phone."

"Huh." Rocky frowned. "I'll let the investigators know and see if we can track him down. He was working on the Valencia house when Kathy was still living there, right?"

Ben answered. "I remember him being there when I picked Kathy up for our date." His face flushed crimson and he looked sideways at me.

A young officer in uniform walked up holding another clear plastic bag. This one appeared to have a driver's license in it—no, multiple driver licenses, I saw once he got closer. He asked Rocky, "Who's handling these?"

"Give them to me. I'll pass them on to Esposito," Rocky answered.

Just then, Birdie Lemon and Stan Lieberman came barreling across the narrow park toward us in a flurry of well-coiffed hair and expensive cologne.

"We heard the terrible news!" Birdie said loudly as she approached.

"How did you two..." Rocky started.

"Oh, they know me," Birdie said, waving her hand toward a group of officers whose backs were turned near the perimeter.

Rocky growled, "This is a crime scene. You need to leave."

As Birdie and Rocky faced off, I watched Stan's eyes slide toward the bag full of driver licenses.

Birdie and Stan showing up here was suspicious, and Stan's focus on the evidence bag was setting off my internal alarms. "I'm Ali," I said loudly, putting my hand out toward Stan, hoping to get his attention off the licenses.

He jumped, and for the briefest moment his face held a flicker of embarrassment. He schooled his expression into the friendly face I remember from the salon. He took my hand and shook it so limply, it was like shaking hands with a dead fish.

"I saw you at the salon yesterday afternoon," I continued.

Recognition dawned on Stan's face. "Ah yes! I remember you. Corey did your nails." He crossed his arms over his soft belly. "Birdie was pretty upset with you."

"Oh, I hope she didn't take that personally," I said, lilting my voice and shooing my hand. "I'm just curious what happened the night poor, dear Mrs. Valencia was killed. She was murdered right next to where I live, you know. Terrible thing."

"Yes," Stan said carefully. "Terrible." His eyebrows dropped and suspicion shadowed his features.

Scrambling to hide my deeper interest and get more information out of Stan, I did what any smart woman does when confronted by a man bathed in cologne. I asked him about himself.

"So how long have you lived in Santa Fe?" I asked. I could see out of the corner of my eye that Ben was watching Rocky and Birdie's interaction, so I felt safe enough letting my attention shift fully to Stan.

Stan's demeanor instantly changed, as I had expected it would. His shoulders relaxed and he shifted his weight to one leg, jutting his hip out. "I've been here for 10 years next month," he shared. "Moved the salon to Paseo De Peralta two years ago, and I'm loving it." His hands were as expressive as his charmingly animated face.

"I hear you have quite a talent," I said, keeping him focused on me. I prayed that Ben was listening closely to Rocky's conversation with Birdie so he could fill me in later. "What could you do with this mop?" I pulled a lock of my straight, bleached hair down in front of my eyes. "I pulled out the color a few weeks ago, and I haven't decided what shade I want. As you can see, my roots are growing in and I'm starting to look a mess!"

Stan leaned toward me. "Do you mind?" he asked as he reached toward my head.

"Go right ahead," I said, tilting the top of my head at him.

He ran his fingers through my hair, flipping it this way and that. "Natural blond. That makes things easier." He put his hand under my chin and tilted it up. "With your fair skin and blue eyes, lavender might look nice. Have you ever had a pastel shade before?"

I nodded. "I've dyed it a few shades of blue, but never lavender. I agree, that might look nice."

Birdie stomped over, gasping as one of her kitten heels got stuck in the grass under her feet. "Sorry to interrupt," she said to Stan with wide eyes that screamed *I need to talk to you*. The woman wasn't subtle. "But we need to finish our planning. Shall, we, dear?" Birdie hooked her arm around Stan's elbow.

"What are you planning?" I asked, not intending for the question to come out so bluntly. *Smooth, Ali*, I admonished myself.

Birdie looked me up and down. "A private affair," she answered pointedly. With that, she pulled Stan toward her and off they walked back through the park toward West Alameda St.

Stan called over his shoulder. "Make an appointment and we'll get that hair taken care of!"

Ben sidled up to me and nodded toward his car when I made eye contact. I nodded back.

The air conditioning was already cooling the Honda's interior when I slid into the passenger seat. I turned the vents so they blasted my face and

I closed my eyes in the cold breeze. I wondered if I would ever get used to the bone-dry heat of New Mexico.

Ben pulled out of the parking spot and onto the road. "Well that was...entertaining," he said.

"Entertaining? How?"

"Rocky and Birdie's dynamic is straight out of a bad romance novel."

I turned my whole body to face Ben. "Excuse me? You do remember he's married to my best friend."

He quickly clarified. "I mean that it's intense. Dramatic."

"It's clear they have a history," I said, calming down a bit. "Do you know anything about it?"

"A little. Rocky's family settled here from Mexico a couple generations back. The Romeros are old-timers in this town, just like the Valencia family. But unlike the Valencias, Rocky's family was quick to sell their land as real-estate developers became interested in Santa Fe as an investment and started scooping up properties. When Birdie moved here and started her firm, one of the first properties she acquired was Rocky's grandfather's old machine shop. Rocky believes Birdie took advantage of a kind old man. While I agree Mr. Romero sold his property on the cheap, I don't think he did it unknowingly. He was ready to retire, and Birdie was ready with a check."

"Rocky's grandfather got screwed? Yeah, that explains why he dislikes Birdie so much," I said.

Ben shook his head. "He didn't get screwed. At least, not in a legal sense. Birdie paid his asking price, and it was enough for him to retire comfortably to a senior center near Taos. But Rocky found out how much Birdie paid for the old auto body shop next door, and felt like Birdie should have paid his grandfather a lot more." He sighed. "That's what he'll tell you, at least. As his friend, I think there's some deeper stuff going on there. I think Rocky expected to take over the machine shop when his grandfather retired."

"I had no idea Rocky was interested in...what do they even *do* at a machine shop?" I asked, feeling heartbroken for my friend.

"Well, *this* machine shop made custom metal shelving and support systems to display heavy artwork like sculptures. Sometimes Mr. Romero would build parts for artists' creations, too. Did you see the Anatomy of Time installation outside the New Mexico Museum of Art on any of your trips here?"

"Yeah, actually I did. I was sad to hear they'd moved it to Los Angeles."

"Mr. Romero manufactured some of those large gears in his shop when the artist was building the installation about seven years back," Ben said as he pulled his car into the parking lot at his apartment complex.

"Impressive," I said. "And that's the kind of thing Rocky wanted to do? As far as I knew, he'd always wanted to be a cop."

Ben turned to me. "I don't know the whole truth of it. I met Rocky when I was at the Academy, and as long as I've known him, he's always been dedicated to law enforcement. I wonder if it's just that the option is now completely off the table for him, and he had no say in it. I don't know. All I can say for sure is he hates Birdie with a fiery passion."

I considered what Ben was saying. I'd known Rocky for eight years, but our friendship was surface-level. Whenever I'd visit, I spent all my time with Bianca. I couldn't even think of more than one or two occasions where I was alone with

Rocky for more than a few minutes. Suddenly he seemed like a total stranger.

He was another man I took for granted.

I cleared my throat. "So, what were they arguing about at the park?"

"Birdie wanted to know what had happened, since that stretch of the park backs up to an apartment complex she owns. Rocky said she was contaminating the crime scene and threatened to have her forcefully removed. What were you talking to Stan about?"

"My hair," I answered simply. I smiled when Ben made a face at me. "Seriously, I was talking to him about my hair. He was trying to scope out those licenses in the evidence bag—he was being so obvious about it. I had a hunch that Stan and Birdie were up to no good, so I distracted him with my lovely locks." I flipped my hair with a flourish.

Ben laughed, then suddenly grew somber. "I can't believe she's dead," he said.

"Kathy? Yeah, that's such a strange turn of events."

"I feel...sorry for her. I mean, she freaked me out, but...I don't think it was completely her fault. I think she was troubled."

"You don't throw yourself off a balcony, break half the bones in your body, and then run out of the hospital if you're mentally healthy," I said, trying to reassure him. "I didn't know her as well as you did, but troubled is probably an understatement."

I heard ringing coming from my purse. I dug around in the overstuffed bag for my phone.

"It's Bianca," I said to Ben, stepping out of the car to take the call.

"Any news on the murder front?" she asked.

"Which murder?" I half joked. "They seem to be popping up all around me in this town."

"Wait, who else died?" Bianca asked.

"Kathy."

"Holy cow."

"Yeah. Ben and I just came from the scene," I shared. "They're not sure if it was a suicide or if there was foul play."

"Rocky's shift doesn't end for another few hours, and he probably won't call me while he's working," Bianca said. "Come over at about 5:00 and fill me in on everything. I'll feed you."

# CHAPTER EIGHTEEN

———

I said a swift goodbye to Ben and headed home to continue packing until it was time to go to Bianca's. Feeling frustrated and tired, I approached my front door, key in hand—and heard voices coming from inside. My heart raced as I turned the handle and found it unlocked. I pushed the door open and found Tom inside with someone I didn't recognize.

"...and it includes the utilities," Tom said to the young man standing next to him in my living room.

"What is going on here?" I demanded, glaring at Tom.

"I'm showing the property. Obviously," Tom responded, glaring right back.

The young man seemed uncomfortable with the exchange. His dull eyes flitted around the room.

"I still live here," I said. I dropped my purse on the floor inside the door, opened the door wider and pointed the way out.

"And I still own this property," Tom said, crossing his arms.

I turned to the young man, who was inching his way around me. "How much is he asking? I'm happy to share what *I'm* paying, if you're interested."

The man stopped in his tracks, his shaggy brown hair falling in his eyes. He opened his mouth to respond and Tom cut him off.

"Let me go ahead and get you an application," Tom said, shooing the man out of my house.

I smirked at Tom and his mouth twisted in an ugly scowl.

I slammed the door behind the two men. A quick walk around didn't turn up anything strange—nothing was moved, and nothing was missing. Tom had no reason to touch my belongings that I could think of, but I didn't trust the man as far as I could throw him.

I plopped down onto my couch and surveyed the sea of boxes in front of me. Was this my future? Moving out of the place I thought I could start over, the place I thought I could build a career that meant something—probably moving in with my parents in California because I didn't have enough money left to make a start anywhere else.

And I kept digging myself in deeper.

Tears stung my eyes. I had thought that finding out who killed Mrs. Valencia would be enough to make Tom give me a break, to move him to let me stay here under the current (low rent) lease agreement. But I couldn't manage to have a single polite encounter with him. I couldn't put my pride aside for a hot second to be nice to him. Even if I solved this murder—and who was I kidding, I was no detective—would it be enough? Had I done too much damage?

I stood up and started walking toward the door. Maybe if I apologized, maybe if I begged Tom...

I stopped with my hand on the door handle. The man was foul. He didn't deserve my apology. All he deserved was a swift kick to his...

My phone rang, making my decision for me. I pulled the phone out of the purse by the door and checked the caller ID. It was Bianca.

"Need another bottle of tequila?" I joked.

Bianca sobbed. "Can you come over now? Something's happened."

I could hear voices in the background mixed with the crackle of what sounded like police radios. "Are you okay?"

"I'm fine." Bianca sniffed. "Just a little scared. I went out to my car to go to the store, and I found someone inside it."

"What?!" I put my hand over my mouth and took a deep breath through my nose. "Did they hurt you?"

"No, no. Nothing like that. It was a man; he was wearing a ski mask and he was going through the car. When he saw me, he ran."

"Are the police there?"

"Yeah. Rocky is here too. I'm really okay. But Rocky has to go back to headquarters and I don't want to be alone."

"I'm on my way."

§

I drove my Jeep like a maniac and made it to

Bianca's house in record time. There were still three police cars parked out front when I got there, in addition to Rocky's unmarked car in the driveway. I could see that Bianca's black Kia Stinger had a broken passenger side window—with it parked next to Rocky's black Charger, I also noticed for the first time that the two cars looked rather similar.

I parked across the street just as two of the three police cars drove off.

I didn't bother to knock. When I walked into the living room, Bianca was sitting on the couch between Rocky and a pile of used tissues. She blew her nose and added a tissue to the pile.

When she saw me, she jumped up and threw her arms around my neck. "Thank you for coming so quickly!"

"Of course," I said. "I only wish I'd been here when it happened. Are you okay?" I took Bianca by the arm and led her back over to the couch. She sat down and leaned into Rocky, who put his arm around her.

"I'm okay," she said, putting her head on her husband's shoulder. "They got here quick." She nodded at an officer I hadn't noticed sitting at the kitchen table with a laptop. The woman had her back to us, and all I could see other than her uniform was a blond head of hair pulled back into a tight bun.

"She's not okay," Rocky corrected. "She's still shaking like a leaf." He squeezed her tighter.

My heart ached at the affection I was witnessing. I sat down on the overstuffed yellow chair across from the couch. The living room was small, and the chair seemed amusingly large in the space and overly bright against the white walls.

"I'll stay with her," I said, nodding at Rocky. "I've got her. Go do what you need to do."

"I don't want to leave, but I want to make sure this report is done right. The thief was going through paperwork in the car—he didn't touch anything of real value, just rifled through papers. With all the strange things happening around here lately...I just want the record to be accurate and thorough. In case there are any connections."

The officer at the table cleared her throat and turned halfway in her chair to face us. Her profile was hawk-like, with a Roman nose and a small chin.

"I know you're going to do a great job, Annette,"

Rocky said to the woman. "But this is my home, and my wife's car, and I am going to be able to add more detail than you can."

The officer nodded and turned back to her laptop. She closed it with a click and slid it into a black leather bag that rested against the leg of the chair she was sitting on. When she stood, so did Rocky.

Bianca and I walked Rocky and the other officer to the door. I could see that it was hard for Bianca to let her husband go—she clung to his arm until he was halfway out the door.

After closing the door behind Rocky, Bianca turned her big, dark eyes to me. "That was scary."

I put my arm around her shoulder and guided her into the kitchen. "I'm sure it was." I nudged her into a seat at the kitchen table. "Any idea what he was looking for?"

"No," she said, shaking her head. "Like Rocky said, he was looking through papers—going through the glovebox and a couple of manila folders I had in there. The tequila is up there." Bianca stood up from the table and pointed to a tall cabinet next to the fridge.

I smiled. Ever since college, a margarita has been

Bianca's answer to everything. I remembered the cabinet where she pulled the margarita glasses from the last time we'd made drinks, and I started to get one out of the cupboard.

"No." Bianca shook her head. "A shot glass, please." She leaned on the counter that separated the kitchen from the nook where the table was.

I frowned. "This guy really shook you up." I pulled down a tall glass for me and a shot glass for her.

Bianca nodded. Her head dropped and her dark hair fell like a curtain around her face. "Being married to a police officer...I guess I'm not afraid of much. I never thought someone would try something like that *here*."

I poured tequila into the shot glass and handed it to Bianca, then I filled my glass with water from the tap. She took the shot in one gulp and held out the glass for another round. I obliged.

"I get it," I said. "Your confidence was shattered."

"Exactly." She set the now-empty shot glass down, took a deep breath and tucked her hair behind her ears. She looked like a troubled child in that moment.

"I can relate to that," I said, leaning against the counter and sipping my water. "I know it's not the same, but when I caught Alex in bed with...well, I still feel like I can't trust my instincts. Like whatever I'm feeling is automatically wrong. I had total confidence in him, in her, in my gut, in my ability to spot lies. I should have seen that coming."

Bianca shook her head. "You loved him. And you believed in her—you were her mentor. You're human, and sometimes humans don't see the connections right in front of their eyes."

That statement triggered something in my memory. "You said the thief was looking for documents in your car," I said. "That reminds me, Stan and Birdie showed up at the park today where Kathy was found dead. Stan was overly interested in an evidence bag full of driver licenses."

"Wait, *Birdie and Stan* crashed a crime scene? Together?"

"Yeah, I thought it was odd too."

"What is with those two?" Bianca asked. She picked up the empty shot glass and turned it over in her hand before holding it out to me.

I thought three shots of straight tequila—the good stuff—was a bit much for someone as small as

Bianca. But I wasn't about to argue with her about it. Not right now. I poured the shot.

"I'm beginning to get more and more suspicious of them," I said. "The more I learn about them...well, they're an odd pair to begin with, aren't they?"

Bianca tilted her head. "As far as I know, they've never traveled in the same circles. They're not friends. I mean, I'm no Santa Fe socialite, and I could be wrong, but I'm pretty well plugged-in here these days...and I agree, they're an odd pair."

"When I was at the salon, I overheard them planning something. Corey told me Stan is known for doing hair for events, so I assumed they were planning an event of some kind...but after today, I wonder." I put my glass in the sink, then snatched Bianca's empty shot glass off the counter and put it in the sink as well before she could ask for another round.

She crossed her arms on the counter and rested her forehead against them. "I should probably eat something," she said, her voice so muffled I almost couldn't make out her words.

"I agree," I said. "Let's see what we've got."

Rummaging through Bianca's small kitchen, I

was able to put together the ingredients for a simple pasta meal. I forced a few glasses of water on my friend as I cooked, and by the time dinner was ready, she had perked up a bit.

We were sitting at the table, shoveling noodles into our mouths. I almost spit out my fettuccine when Bianca said, "What if we set up a sting to find out what Birdie and Stan are up to."

"No more tequila for you." I laughed.

"I'm serious!" Bianca insisted. "You said it yourself, they're acting suspicious." She rested her fork on the edge of her bowl and sat back in her chair. "I don't want you to leave. You just got here." Her voice was sad, and for the second time that evening she reminded me of a child.

"I don't want to leave either." I sighed. "And I *really* don't want to have to move in with my parents."

Bianca's head snapped up. "Your *parents*? I didn't realize that was your plan. How are you...how are you going to survive that? After what happened at graduation..."

I took another bite, chewed and swallowed before I could muster up an answer. "I don't know. I don't even know if they'll let me stay with them.

It just seems like the best backup plan for now. Something to aim at." I took a deep breath. "I'm meeting Birdie's husband tomorrow for a portrait consultation. I don't think it's going to work out—I just get a PITA vibe from him..."

"PITA vibe?" Bianca asked.

"Pain in the...rear," I explained. "I've worked with enough clients over the years—not portrait clients necessarily, but marketing and advertising clients—that I can recognize red flags pretty quickly. Lots of red flags with this guy."

"But if he pays you well, wouldn't that mean you could stay?"

"Only if I can convince him to pay me up front. Portraits take a lot of time. At least a month, and that's if he's open to me using acrylic paint. If he insists on an oil painting—it could be a two- or three-month project." I shook my head at my plate, suddenly not hungry. "And I'm running out of savings fast."

Bianca scraped the bottom of her bowl with her fork, and I winced at the awful sound. She didn't notice my reaction. She seemed lost in thought.

"I'm going to find a way to keep you here," she

finally said with a stubborn upward tilt of her chin. "You came all this way because of me..."

I cut her off. "Yes, I came all this way because of you—in the best possible sense. When I caught Alex in bed with Cindy—in *my* bed with Cindy—I felt like I had nothing. The career I'd built in Chicago, the amazing apartment I shared with Alex, the relationship I was sure was going to last forever...it was gone in an instant. My home wasn't safe anymore. My job wasn't either—Alex worked in the same building and Cindy was my assistant at the agency, for goodness sake."

Bianca put her hand on top of mine. I hadn't realized I was gripping the edge of the table. I fought back a sob. "When you invited me here, and you even found a place for me to live, you weren't just giving me hope that it might be possible to pursue my dreams of being a full-time artist...you gave me a new home."

I took a deep breath to steady myself before continuing. "I'm the one who messed it up. My predicament is *not* your fault. I was rude to Tom right from the get-go, and not only did I never try to fix that, I have made it worse every time I've run into him. I don't know why, but something about him just gets to me. I turn into a tactless, angry bit..."

Bianca smacked my arm. "Maybe you're projecting. Maybe Tom reminds you of Alex in some way and you're punishing him because you can't punish Alex."

"Putting your psychology degree to work?" I laughed.

"Gotta use that college education where I can." Bianca laughed, too.

A moment passed in silence, and Bianca continued more softly. "You've been through a lot this year. It was incredibly brave of you to leave your life in Chicago and move across the country to a town where you knew only two people. It was even braver of you to try to pursue your dreams of being a professional artist. And you did it without hesitation. You just left your job, packed your things and went for it. I don't think I could ever be so brave."

I snorted. "Reckless is more like it."

"You can do this, you know." Bianca's dark brown eyes were pleading.

"Do what?"

"Make it here. You're talented. And brave. If

anyone can make it as an artist in this town, you can."

I shook my head. "I guess I'll never know. In a few weeks, I'll have just enough money left for one more move—but Tom will make sure I'm out of the Little House long before then."

Bianca smiled wickedly. "Unless we catch his mother's killer and he's so grateful that he lets you stay."

I chuckled. "That was the plan. But I haven't had much success playing detective so far."

My phone chirped on the counter behind me, and I reached up and grabbed it. "It's your husband," I said to Bianca.

She put her hand to her heart and gasped dramatically. "What is my husband doing texting my best friend? Is there something you want to tell me, Ali?"

I rolled my eyes. "He sent me three pictures of driver licenses with a message asking if I recognize any of them from Kathy's place." I looked them over. I didn't recognize the licenses from Kathy's hostel room—but the pictures on them *were* familiar. I felt certain I had seen all three of those men at the main house at Villa Valencia the day I arrived.

I wrote back: LOOK LIKE DAVID'S CREW. AT THE MAIN HOUSE ON THURSDAY.

His message back was a short THANKS.

"I wonder if those licenses were found with Kathy's body earlier today. I told you Stan was nosing around the evidence bag full of driver licenses."

"And the licenses belong to David's crew?"

"I could be wrong, but they looked identical to the men I saw at Villa Valencia working with David the day I arrived," I said. "And David is currently missing—or so Aaron believes. He hasn't been showing up for jobs, and no one can reach him." I snapped my fingers. "The belt that Rocky had me come identify today that was found next to Kathy—that looked just like the belt I saw David wearing at the gallery yesterday. David must be mixed up in this somehow."

"Curiouser and curiouser," Bianca said. She pressed her lips together. "I still think we need to set up a sting. Find out what Stan and Birdie are up to. If they came nosing around, I'll bet they know something." She gasped suddenly and slammed her hands on the table. "What if they had something to do with my car getting broken into today? The thief was clearly looking for some kind of paperwork or document or something."

"Well, your car does look an awful lot like Rocky's, too. I was wondering if there might be a connection there." I looked sideways at my friend, pushed my chair back, which scraped horribly on the wood floor, and crossed my arms. "There's no way I'm talking you out of a sting, anyway, am I."

Bianca crossed her arms too. "Nope."

"All right. Well, better I join you to keep you out of trouble."

Bianca's face lit up in a satisfied smile. "Great. I've got just the plan."

# CHAPTER NINETEEN

———

Later that night, we were tucked into the small nook at the back of the Desert Wind Boutique where the dressing rooms were located.

"How did you get them to agree to come here tonight?" I whispered to Bianca.

"Sshh!" she warned, pointing to one of the dressing rooms. I threw her an annoyed look and entered the small changing room.

Bianca pulled the curtain closed, then stuck her face through the crack between the curtain and the wall. "I'll tell you later." She turned her head, looking out to the retail floor. "I'll get them as close to the back here as I can, and I'll get them talking. Then I'll putter about so they don't think I'm listening. You hit record on your phone as soon as they start talking."

As Bianca walked away, I slid down onto the small bench inside the dressing room. I wondered if this "sting" was something she learned from Rocky...or something she saw in a bad murder-mystery cable show.

I heard Bianca's sing-song voice greeting someone, but I couldn't make out any words—from her or the person she was greeting. They were too far away.

A moment later, I heard another sound. This time it was someone shuffling around just outside the dressing room nook. My heartbeat quickened. What if they pulled back the curtain and saw me there? What would my excuse be? I looked down. I was wearing a light knit multicolored shawl over a black tank top. *I can take this off and if someone peeks in here I can act like I was just about to get changed!* I set the phone down on the bench to make my move—and it was much louder than I meant for it to be. I froze.

The sounds outside the dressing room ceased.

"Is someone there?" a man's voice asked in a loud whisper. It sounded like Stan.

It went quiet again. After a minute of silence, I could breathe. I hadn't been caught.

"Stan!" This time the voice was distinctly Birdie's, and I jumped at the sound.

"What are you doing here?" Stan asked.

"Well I can ask you the same thing," she said harshly.

"Bianca asked me to come here for an updo consultation," Stan said. I couldn't see his face—I couldn't see anything at all other than the red curtain in front of me—but his voice sounded annoyed. "Apparently her shop is going to be in the news tomorrow, and she doesn't want her hair to distract from her merchandise."

"Makes sense," Birdie said in a thoughtful tone. Or was it an unbelieving tone? Without seeing her face, I couldn't tell.

"And you? Why are *you* here?" Stan asked.

Birdie answered, "Bianca told me she has some inside information on the Valencia property."

"And she couldn't tell you over the phone?"

"Hmph. Stan Lieberman, I didn't get where I am by knowing what everyone else knows. I get the scoop so I can make the best deal. And you don't get a *scoop* over the phone. Who knows who's listening in on a phone call?" Birdie's voice was both confident and dismissive. It was an ugly combination.

Suddenly, I remembered my phone. I hit the record button.

"You don't think she knows..." Stan started.

"Of course she doesn't know," Birdie hissed. There was silence for another few heartbeats. "I found a new forger for the documents," she said in such a quiet voice, I almost couldn't make out what she said. "Carmen isn't going anywhere."

Bianca's voice piped up. "Birdie, can I talk to you alone for a moment? Stan, I was thinking that wall over there as the backdrop. Can you take a look and start getting ideas while I talk to Birdie? It'll just take a second."

A moment went by, then Bianca continued. "Tom has been actively showing the Little House. You know he's evicting Ali, right? It doesn't look like he's planning to sell. And this is just between you and me, but I heard through the grapevine that Mrs. Valencia put a stipulation in the will that if he sold the property to *you*, he'd have to give the profits to charity."

"Why that horrible...!" Birdie spat. "That old woman had it out for me, and I'll never know why."

*I can take a few guesses*, I thought. My rear end was starting to hurt on the hard wooden bench, but I didn't dare move with Bianca and Birdie so close.

"Oh, Stan!" Bianca called—it sounded like her face was pointed away from the back of the store, now. "I just remembered, I have a lovely selection of scarves we can add to that. I'll get them from the back."

Silence again.

"Well?" Stan whispered.

"That old bat is still screwing me over, even from the grave," Birdie whispered back. She quickly filled Stan in on what Bianca had just told her.

"At least you can rest easy knowing we made her pay," Stan said.

My overstuffed purse chose that moment to fall over on the bench next to me, and it knocked my phone to the floor with a loud thump before I could catch it.

Birdie threw open the curtain and stared at me, open mouthed. "You!"

I grabbed my phone and purse and made a run

for it, bumping Stan into a rack of clothes as I scrambled past. I weaved my way as quickly as I could through the maze of clothing racks and display stands, my heart racing.

I burst through the doors of the boutique into the cool night air and didn't stop until I stumbled into an alley on the other side of the plaza. I leaned against a white plaster wall, huffing and puffing. I couldn't catch my breath. My heart was racing so fast, I felt like I might pass out.

*Get a grip, Ali.* I focused on slowing my breath until I could breathe through my nose again. Then I counted—inhale to the count of five, exhale to the count of six. It was a technique I learned from a meditation and mindfulness instructor I met in my college days in Boulder, and it never failed to calm me down.

Yet right now, it was failing me.

I had just recorded what could be a murder confession.

I looked down at the phone in my hand—I hadn't even put it in my purse as I was running across downtown trying to escape. There were three text messages from Bianca.

*Oh my God. Bianca.* I left her with the murderer! *What is* wrong *with me?!*

I called her. My hands were shaking. I couldn't breathe.

She didn't answer the shop phone.

I called her cell phone.

No answer.

I called the shop phone again.

Three rings, and she picked up. "Desert Wind, how may I help you?"

"Bianca! Are you okay?" I shrieked into the receiver.

"I'm fine! Are *you* okay?" she answered, sounding relieved.

"Yes, I'm okay. I'm coming back."

"No. Stay where you are. I'll come to you."

I described the location of the alley I was hiding out in, and Bianca seemed to know it immediately. Ten minutes ticked by achingly slowly as I waited for her in the alley. Finally, I saw her distinct silhouette backlit by the streetlamp across from the alley entrance. I waved her over.

"They both took off the second you ran past," she said as she hugged me tight. "I was so scared that they'd chased after you, I called Rocky. He's on his way."

"I don't know if they chased after me," I said in a shaking voice. "I ran as fast as I could, and I never looked back until I got to this alley."

Bianca tilted her head at the wall behind me. "Good choice. This place has excellent martinis."

I laughed.

Rocky's Charger pulled up and blocked the entrance to the alley. He got out and ran to his wife. "Are you okay?"

"I'm fine," Bianca answered. She nodded at me. "We're both fine. And we're pretty sure we caught Mrs. Valencia's murderer."

Bianca filled in Rocky on everything that had happened that night. I played the recording on my phone for him to corroborate her story.

"That doesn't sound good," he said. "But it's not proof."

"Isn't it enough to bring him in for questioning, though?" I asked.

"You watch too many murder mysteries. Just like my wife." Rocky nudged Bianca. "But yeah, I'll bring him in."

I breathed a sigh of relief. My first easy breath all night.

# CHAPTER TWENTY

———

The next morning, I was a nervous wreck. I was supposed to meet Lawrence Lemon for his portrait consultation—and I had just recorded his wife admitting to Mrs. Valencia's murder. Maybe. The more I thought about the conversation I overheard last night, the more doubts I had.

I got dressed in my most no-nonsense ensemble: dark, skin-tight jeans, a black tank top, and black ankle boots. With my platinum hair, I knew the outfit made me look foreboding.

My mind wandered as I finished the look with a swipe of blood-red lipstick. No matter how poorly Lawrence got along with his wife, Birdie, he couldn't possibly be okay with what I did. I thought about not going to the meeting. I thought about calling his assistant and telling him I was sick. In the end, curiosity and money won out.

Oddly, while I was nervous to meet Lawrence, I was also glad to have the distraction. The events of the night before were on a loop in my brain, and I couldn't stop wondering if Rocky had picked up Stan yet. I'm sure he'd tell me as soon as he could—but it wouldn't be soon enough.

I was so lost in thought driving to Lawrence's firm, I almost missed the turn-in for the parking lot at the large, almost sinister-looking building. I braked quickly and turned in, glancing in my rearview mirror to make sure my poor driving wasn't going to get me rear-ended. Luckily there was no one behind me.

I parked in an empty spot, got out of the Jeep and peered up at the building. It was three stories high, and from what I read on the firm's website, Lemon, Trinidad and Associates took up the entire third floor.

The building was the first one over two stories tall that I'd seen in Santa Fe, but that wasn't the only reason it stuck out like cactus in a cotton field. All concrete and angles, it looked more like a prison than an office building. I wondered what hoops the developer had to jump through to get a permit for a building like that with how much power the historic preservation division had over the aesthetics of this city.

I made my way through the heavy glass door in the front of the building. The foyer was even more intimidating than the exterior. The room was lined with large oil paintings of older men in suits. A large cherrywood reception desk sat in the center of the black-and-white tiled floor, and a prim-looking woman with a French twist in her mahogany hair looked up from her seat behind the counter.

"May I help you?" the woman asked, pushing her glasses halfway down her nose to look at me over the rim.

"I'm here to see Lawrence Lemon."

"Name?" she asked.

"Ali Porter," I said. My voice echoed in the stern-looking room.

The woman pushed her glasses back up on her nose and picked up the phone. "One moment," she said, dialing a number.

I stepped back from the desk and fidgeted while

she spoke to whoever it was on the other end of the line. I felt uncomfortable in this place dressed as I was. I wasn't looking to impress this man—in fact, my clothing choices had been meant to intimidate him—and I now I second-guessed myself. I stuck out like a sore thumb.

"Head on up," said the receptionist, pointing toward a bank of elevators to my right.

The ride up was slow, and I wished I had asked where the stairs were instead. When the doors opened on the third floor, a tall, woman with shoulder-length, dirty blond hair stood in front of me, her hands clasped neatly in front of her gray pencil skirt.

"Ali?" the woman asked.

I nodded. She held out a manicured hand to me and I shook it.

"I'm Maggie, Larry's architectural assistant," she said. Then, noticing my confusion, she added, "I'm sure you were expecting Trevor, the *administrative* assistant—but sadly he called in sick this morning. You're stuck with me." She winked. Her startlingly blue eyes then dropped to my hands. "French manicure!" she said, pointing at my nails. She lifted her right hand and showed me her nails.

I smiled and said, "The gal who did my nails told me French manicures are unusual these days."

"Oh, they are. Here, at least. I saw them a lot more back in Chicago."

I beamed at her. "You're from Chicago?"

"Born and raised," she said, waving me into the room.

"I just moved here from Chicago," I said, following her.

"You don't say!" she said, stopping at a shorter, less intimidating reception desk. "I don't meet many people in Santa Fe coming from Chicago."

"I was born and raised in California," I explained. "I went to college in Boulder, Colorado, and took a job in Chicago after I graduated."

"That must have been a culture shock," she said, laughing.

"Not as much of a culture shock as going from Chicago to Santa Fe!" I laughed too.

"I see you've met Maggie," said a man's voice from behind me.

As I turned around to locate the source, Maggie said, "Ali, this is Larry."

The man walking toward me wasn't what I expected. He was average height, but rather wide and heavyset. He looked more like a linebacker than a lawyer. His gray suit was accented by a pink tie, and when he reached out his hand to shake mine, the suit strained at the shoulders.

"Nice to meet you face-to-face," Larry said, shaking my hand firmly. "Thanks for coming on such short notice."

"Do I call you Lawrence or Larry?" I asked, pulling my hand back and resisting the urge to shake it out. The man had one heck of a grip.

"Larry, please. Only my wife and her friends call me Lawrence." He pointed to the hall behind him. "Shall we?"

If the man wasn't what I expected, his office was exactly as I had pictured. White walls, white carpet, beige chairs and a glass-top desk. To the left of the door was a wall of windows overlooking the road below. I could just make out the hills in the distance through the late summer haze.

On the opposite wall was a gas fireplace framed by tile in a checkerboard design alternating white and clear glass tiles.

Larry pointed at the fireplace. "That's where she wants the portrait."

I looked at the man, then the fireplace, then back to the man. "And what do *you* want?"

He chuckled. "Whatever gets her to stay away from my office for a while. Though I'm not even sure *this* is going to do it." He put his hand up to the side of his mouth as if he were about to tell me a secret. "She's sure I'm cheating on her, you know. I think she hangs around here just to try to catch me in the act." He guffawed, his boisterous laughter bouncing off the stark walls.

I couldn't help but laugh with him. His laugh was infectious. I sobered quickly, though. "Larry...about your wife. Last night I did something..."

Larry put his hand up, stopping my speech before it began. "I know. I heard. I got a good laugh out of it, to be honest. Birdie expects everyone in this town to be under her spell, and when the odd person comes along who doesn't bow under her rule..." he put both hands in the air and waggled his fingers, "...fireworks. It's a sight to behold." That boisterous laugh exploded from his smiling face once again.

"So she wasn't arrested?" I asked, my eyebrows

so high it felt like they were going to reach the ceiling any moment.

"Arrested? No. Why would she be arrested?" he asked, cocking his head to the side and giving me a quizzical look.

"Well, it sounded like...it sounded like she had something to do with Mrs. Valencia's murder."

Larry doubled over with laughter so loud it shook the walls. When he finally got a hold of himself, he explained, "Birdie, for all her power-grabbing and scheming, is not a murderer. And she wasn't anywhere near Mrs. Valencia's home that night, that's for sure."

I stared at Larry for a long moment, unsure what to say. "I'm sorry," I said finally. "The way she and Stan talked about Mrs. Valencia, I was so sure."

Larry waved his hand at me dismissively. "Don't worry about it. It makes this all the more fun for me. She's going to be furious when she finds out I hired you."

"Well, good art *is* supposed to be provocative." I smiled from ear to ear and he laughed riotously. I liked this man.

"So where do we start?" Larry asked when he'd

regained his composure. He moved to stand to the side of his glass desk.

I looked him up and down. "You don't match."

Larry looked down at his suit. "This is an expensive suit. I hope I match."

"Not your clothes," I said with a light chuckle. "I mean you don't match this office."

He sighed and sat down on the large beige swivel chair behind the desk. "This is Birdie's little design project. I'm just along for the ride."

"But you're the one who has to work here day in and day out," I said. "Don't you want something a little more...you?"

"Well according to my wife, if I had my way, this office would look like a circus tent."

"Tell me more about that," I said. "What sorts of things do you like? Colors, textures, patterns..."

Larry folded his hands behind his head and leaned back in the chair until he was looking at the ceiling. "I like color," he said. "Lots of color. Bold patterns. Designs that are fun...whimsical."

I looked around the room again. This was as far from "whimsical" as you could get.

I felt an internal nudge. "Why did you become an architect?" I asked him.

Larry took his hands out from behind his head and looked at me. "My father was an architect. So was my grandfather. It's tradition." He shrugged. "When I was younger, I dreamed of designing eclectic, colorful buildings that would blend American Southwest style with Mediterranean—really spice up this town. Then my father died and left me in charge of the firm, and I married Birdie...and none of that seemed to matter anymore."

"Dreams always matter," I said softly. "Even if they have to go on hold for a bit, they are a part of you. An important part of you."

I walked to the fireplace and looked up at the big, white space above. "I have an idea," I said. "But I don't think Birdie's going to like it."

# CHAPTER TWENTY-ONE

---

After I wrapped up my portrait consultation with Larry, I went to Bianca's house. As I walked up the driveway toward the front door, I noticed the broken window of her Kia had been covered by clear plastic sheeting.

Bianca opened the door before I could knock. "So?" she asked breathlessly as she swung the door wide open and waved me through.

"So I think I might have solved my money problem," I said.

We went into the living room and I sat on the bright yellow chair across from where Bianca sat on the couch.

I continued, "Larry liked my ideas for his

portrait so much, he agreed to pay half up front...under one condition."

"*Larry?*" Bianca said incredulously. "You're on nickname terms with Lawrence Lemon now?"

I laughed. "He was certainly not what I expected. Have you ever met him?"

"No. I've seen him at parties and gallery openings with Birdie, but I've never properly met him."

"He's...nice. Friendly. Kind. Not what I'd expect from someone married to Birdie."

"Rumor has it that it was something of an 'arranged marriage.'" Bianca shared. "Lawrence—Larry—was too focused on work to date much, and his father wanted him to have someone after he was gone. Robert Lemon, Larry's father, had the kind of cancer you don't expect to live through."

My heart ached. Poor Larry, to watch his father die like that...and poor Robert, to know he was going to die and just want someone to take care of his son.

"What was the condition that Larry had for you, when he agreed to pay you up-front for the portrait?" Bianca asked, getting the conversation back on track.

"He wants me to come to the party Birdie is hosting with the SFPAA at a gallery downtown on Friday," I answered, tucking my hair behind my ear. "It sounds...fancy."

Bianca slapped her hand over her mouth. "That's an invite-only event. Rocky and I will be there, and Felicia will be too—I would have gotten you a ticket if I could have, but they were hard to come by, and crazy expensive. And now you can come with us! I'm so happy!" She was practically squealing.

"Not so fast. Do you remember last night? Birdie probably hates me." I shuddered.

"She hates everyone. Welcome to the club. Besides, it was Stan who confessed to the murder..."

"We think," I corrected her.

"It's so obvious! And if Birdie knew about it—well, she'll be arrested, and she won't even be at the party."

"About that..." I started before I was cut off.

"YOU TWO," Rocky's voice boomed across the house. He stormed into the living room, hands on hips. "Stan's alibi is airtight. He didn't kill Mrs. Valencia. But he is talking about suing the two of you for entrapment. Or libel. Or false accusation—he went on for an hour about all the things he's going to sue you for."

Bianca frowned. "He didn't sue Mrs. Valencia, and she went around town badmouthing him so bad he lost business."

"He was in the process of suing her," Rocky said. He shook his head. "That is one lawsuit-happy hairdresser. You two need to *butt out*. You're only making things worse."

"What about what Stan said about making her pay?" I argued.

"*Airtight* alibi, Ali," Rocky repeated.

"And what Birdie said about a forger and someone named Carmen?"

"Carmen is Birdie's housekeeper. And Birdie insists she said 'corner for the Dali painting'—not 'forger for the documents.'" Rocky said with a sigh. "Even with the audio enhanced by our tech team, we can't verify what she said. She said it too quietly."

*Oh, this is the last thing I need.* I stood up, "So we're back to square one—no suspects, a murderer on the loose—and now I'm going to get sued." Tears welled in my eyes. I turned away from my friends so they wouldn't see me crying. I wasn't sad, or even angry. I just felt...defeated.

I walked to the front door. Bianca shouted behind me, "Ali, where are you going?"

"To tell Tom he wins." I closed the door behind me a little harder than I meant to.

§

I pounded on the front door of the main house at Villa Valencia at noon. When Tom answered the door, he was dabbing at his mouth with a napkin.

"What do you want?" he snarled. "I'm eating lunch."

"Can I come in?" I asked as politely as I could, even though every bone in my body wanted to be snide right back to him.

"Fine," he said, opening the door wider.

I walked into the living room, toward the El Camino de Rosas painting that still hung over the fireplace. For a flickering instant I wondered if a painting like that could be enough to warm up Larry's stark white office.

I turned to face Tom. "I am here to say I'm sorry."

"Excuse me?" Tom looked at me with his mouth agape.

"I'm sorry. We got off on the wrong foot, and that was probably my fault. I was rude to you every time I met you after that, and that was *definitely* my fault." My pride hurt so bad I thought I was going to throw up.

Tom crushed the napkin in his hand and crossed his hairy arms. "What's your game?"

"No game," I said. "I just wanted to set things right. As best I can, at least."

Tom didn't budge from his position, or say a word.

I sighed. "Look...I don't want to lose the Little House. I can't afford anything else like this in town—a place to live *and* studio space, and at such a low price. And I really want to make my home here." I swallowed. *Here it comes.* "I'll understand if you say no. I deserve that. But would you consider...would you consider letting me stay here under the existing lease agreement?"

Tom stared at me, impassive but visibly triumphant.

"Please," I added. I couldn't look at him while he stared at me with such a victorious expression. My eyes slid to the painting. The light from the half-finished kitchen reflected off the surface of the Camino and glinted in my eye.

At that same moment, I noticed the familiar smell of varnish. I looked closer at the painting. Navarro's brushstrokes were unmistakable. Bold yet gentle. I saw the tiny flecks of blood in the corner of the painting and my stomach clenched.

Tom's voice snapped me out of my train of thought. "No," he said simply.

My shoulders slumped. I looked at the floor. "Okay," I said. "I get it." I started for the door.

"Wait," Tom said. The tone of his voice was different now. "I appreciate your apology. And...I wasn't very nice either. I mean, I had an excuse—my mother was murdered. That's tough to smile through."

I nodded. "I can only imagine."

When it was clear that Tom wasn't going to say anything else, I turned and kept walking toward the door. As I opened it to let myself out, I said to him, "I was trying to solve her murder, you know."

"What?" he asked, still standing in the living room.

I spoke a little louder. "I thought that...I thought that if I could find your mother's killer, you would have to let me stay."

Tom chuckled lightly. "That might've done it," he said. "Good luck, Ali. Be out by the end of the weekend."

# CHAPTER TWENTY-TWO

———

Friday night, I walked up the rough stone steps to the reception hall where the SFPAA party was being held. I held up my long, sparkly blue dress so I wouldn't trip. Glancing down at my hands, I noticed the contrast between the shimmering sapphire dress and my pale skin.

*If my hair were several inches longer, I'd look like Elsa. I've really got to do something about this hair color.* My heart clenched. Stan would never agree to do my hair now, that was for sure. I wondered if Corey could recommend someone else. Then I wondered if I could get to Corey at the salon without running into Stan there.

I had really made some bad impressions on

people in Santa Fe—and I had only been there a week. *I hope I can make things right. If I can find a place to live here, that is.*

I had spent Thursday packing my belongings and moving my whole life into a storage unit. It felt like a huge risk—but it also felt *right*. The deposit and first-month rent on the storage unit took a big chunk of my savings. And without being employed, few landlords in this town would take a chance on me. On top of all that, with rent prices sky-high in this town, I wasn't sure I had enough money left for a deposit on a new place, much less first month's rent. Of course, if Larry kept his word and paid me half my portrait fee for attending this party, that last part should work out just fine.

This all felt like a huge gamble.

But I had a hunch.

And if my hunch paid off tonight, Tom might let me stay after all.

As I walked through the door and into the party, my jaw hit the floor at the scene before me. The ballroom was cavernous. On the far end was a stage with a live band playing 1920s flapper music. Between where I stood and where the stage was, it was a sea of art. Paintings lined every wall.

Sculptures and performance art pieces took up every inch of the floor where there weren't tables and open bars.

"Name, please?" A woman's voice startled me out of my trance. I turned to my right and noticed for the first time a welcome table manned by two middle-aged women. Nametags were neatly lined up on the table's surface, and each woman held a clipboard.

"Ali Porter. *Alissandra* Porter," I corrected myself.

The woman on the left checked my name off her list, then stood over the assortment of nametags. I noticed they were in alphabetical order by first name, and pointed at my nametag before the woman was able to spot it. She picked it up and handed it to me across the table.

"As I'm sure you know, this is a charity event. Twenty-five percent of the proceeds from any art purchases will go to the SFPAA, and 25 percent will go to Angel House, the local women's shelter," the woman explained as I pinned my nametag on my dress.

"And where does the other 50 percent go?" I

asked absentmindedly as I struggled to close the pin.

"To the artist, of course," the woman asked with an eye-roll.

"Of course," I responded. *Wow, the SFPAA sure is a friendly group. I'm sure Birdie fits right in.*

As if on cue, Birdie walked up to the welcome table and addressed the other woman there who was still seated. "Be sure to let me know if anyone tries to get in without a..." Then she noticed I was standing there. "Oh, *you.*" She looked at the women manning the welcome table. "This is what I'm talking about. If someone tries to enter without being on the list—like *this*—" She pointed at me. "Radio security and we'll have them escorted out."

My cheeks flushed and I was grateful for the dim lighting of the entryway. I cleared my throat. "I have an invitation, Birdie." I pointed at my nametag.

"That's impossible," she said, crossing her arms over her red, cap-sleeved dress.

Larry walked up behind his wife and put his arm around her. "I invited her," he said. He stood about an inch shorter than Birdie, who was in high heels—but he was easily three times as wide as her.

"What? *Why?*" Birdie asked Larry, pushing his arm off her shoulders and turning to face him.

"I like her," he answered simply. He shrugged. "She had some great ideas for my portrait. You know, the portrait you so desperately want me to have in my office?" His smile turned into a smirk.

"Out of all the artists in town you could have chosen, why would you choose *this woman*, who tried to have me arrested?"

"I didn't try to have *you* arrested." I tried to correct her, but she held up a finger to shush me.

"She came highly recommended..." he started.

"By whom?" Birdie asked pointedly.

"Felicia Barnes," he answered.

Birdie rolled her eyes. "Of course. Felicia. I should have guessed. Doesn't matter. Ali can't be here."

"Why not?" Larry asked.

I felt like an intruder watching this exchange, but there was no way I could sneak past them and out into the party without Birdie noticing me and screaming for security.

"Because she's not a member of this community. This is a *community* event." Birdie's voice was getting higher and louder.

"This is a charity event, actually. And there are plenty of people from outside the community here tonight. Like the Darwins over there." Larry nodded to a couple admiring a painting on the far wall. "And Casey Chavez." Larry pointed to a man standing not too far from the Darwins, talking to Aaron Taylor animatedly near a performance art piece that included a naked woman draped over a gilded throne.

My eyes locked on Aaron, and as if he could feel my gaze, he looked up and met my eyes. He nodded at me without smiling.

"I bought her ticket," Larry continued, "because I enjoy her company, I think she's a great addition to this community—" he emphasized that word, driving his point home, "—and I want her opinion on some pieces I'm looking at here tonight."

Larry stepped toward me and extended his elbow, an invitation for me to take it. "Would you do me the honor of being my art consultant tonight?"

"I..." I stammered.

"*She's* not the one you're having an affair with, is she? *Her?*" Birdie screeched.

Larry rolled his eyes and nudged his elbow

toward me again. I put my arm through his, just hoping to get away from this scene. He patted my hand resting on his forearm. "I could only be so lucky," he said, smiling kindly at me.

Birdie stomped her high-heeled foot as we walked away.

"I hope inviting me here was worth all that drama," I said, my face still hot. I couldn't look at anyone else in the room besides Larry—I was sure everyone was staring.

"To get under Birdie's skin like that? Worth every penny. Besides, I wasn't lying about wanting your opinion. There are a few pieces here I really like, and I worry they're going to clash too much with the new office décor. I wondered if you could give me your opinion on them, and help me figure out how I might make them work in that space."

"I'm not an interior designer. Or an art critic," I argued. "Aaron over there would probably give you better advice."

Larry shook his head. "You *see* me. I'm tired of other people trying to tell me who I am and what I should like." He stopped, pulling me to a stop as well. He looked at the floor. "When you came to my office and I told you the colors and styles I liked, you didn't laugh."

"Why would I laugh?" I asked, shocked. "You like what you like. Everyone is free to like what they like."

"I'm not. At least, I've never been before," Larry said. His eyes finally looked up from the floor, but he didn't look at me—he looked at someone walking toward him.

Stan Lieberman.

Stan was dressed to the nines in a black suit and pink-and-blue checkered bowtie. His frosted hair glowed in the spotlight meant for the painting behind him.

"I should be furious with you," Stan said to me. He crossed his arms over his stomach. "But it turns out, you did me a huge favor."

I opened my mouth to speak, but as stunned as I was, nothing came out.

"When your friend Rocky took me in for questioning, he saw right through my alibi for the night of Mrs. Valencia's murder..." he started.

"But Rocky said your alibi checked out," I blurted.

Stan put up a finger indicating I should stop

talking. "Let me finish. That alibi was fake. He was right. But I didn't murder that rotten old woman." Stan cleared his throat. "Sorry, I shouldn't speak ill of the dead. I didn't murder Mrs. Valencia. And I did have an airtight alibi." He looked at Larry and his eyes softened. "I had just promised not to reveal it." He looked back at me. "I used my one phone call to call Larry, and he told me it was okay. So I told the truth. Larry and I were together that night."

"Together..." I questioned.

"Together," the two men said at once.

"Oooohhhh."

"And tonight, we're telling Birdie," Larry said. "It's all thanks to you."

"Don't tell Birdie I had anything to do with that! Your wife will murder me," I said to Larry as all the blood rushed out of my cheeks.

"I won't let her bother you," Larry said, patting my shoulder. "And she'll be fine. She's built quite an empire of her own in this town. She doesn't need me—or my money—anymore. Honestly, she'll be happier without me."

"I hope you're right," I said with a pinched smile. "Good luck, Larry. You might not want to have that conversation with Birdie at the party tonight, though. She might explode and ruin all this beautiful art." Just then, I saw someone waving at me from near the stage. "Would you excuse me?"

I didn't wait for Larry and Stan to say yes. Feeling like I just emerged from a tornado, I left the two men gazing lovingly into each other's eyes and made my way across the floor to Rocky and Bianca.

"What was all that about?" Bianca asked, stirring her cocktail. She wore a short, black, sleeveless dress accented by a silver tassel on a long chain around her neck. Rocky complemented her in his black suit and silver tie.

"Apparently Larry and Stan are...a thing," I said. Rocky grinned.

"You knew," I stated.

"I told you," he said. "Stan's alibi was airtight."

I sighed. "That still doesn't get us any closer to finding out who murdered my landlord."

Aaron walked up, holding a bottle of craft beer. His suit was a soft blue, and the white shirt underneath was unbuttoned. He looked straight out of the '70s.

"Find anything you like?" Aaron asked us before taking a swig of his beer.

"There are a few pieces I would love to have...but they're out of our price range," Bianca said as she looped her free hand through the crook of Rocky's elbow.

"I haven't had a chance to look around yet," I answered Aaron next.

He nodded in that condescending way I was getting used to. "Is there a certain style you like? I can probably point you to a few pieces."

"That'd be great," I said. "I like traditional southwestern style—landscapes mostly."

"Aren't you a portrait artist?" he asked, looking down his long nose and taking a sip of his beer.

"Yes. Doesn't mean I want a house full of portraits."

"You don't display your own work?" he asked.

"Not in my home, no. Once a painting is complete and dry, it goes into storage until it's either sold or off to a gallery."

I felt like a bit of a fake talking like I had some *process* around how I sold my art. The reality was I had only had one gallery showing in Chicago, and it was a favor from a friend—not because the gallery owner particularly liked my style. And I'd only sold three portraits in my life. All commissions.

But Aaron's snobbery irked me. I didn't want to reveal to this man what an amateur I was.

"Hmm. Okay then. Are you interested in only paintings or are you open to looking at sculptures?" he asked.

"I'm open to looking at beautiful art, period," I said.

Aaron took a drink, then pointed the top of his beer bottle toward a collection of work across the room. "There are a few pieces from Torrance Carson you might like, and a sculpture from Ursula Ambra."

When I nodded my head in response, I looked down at his loafers and noticed that his socks matched—unlike the night I met him. His relaxed demeanor was different, too. The way he arched one eyebrow when he spoke was still snooty as could be, but there was an easy confidence about him tonight.

"Sounds good. But first I need a drink," I said. *I need* multiple *drinks to deal with Aaron.*

Bianca answered my unspoken question. "There's a bar right over there." She pointed to a narrow bar on the other side of the stage from where we stood.

"I'll be right back," I said. I walked off, not giving Aaron a chance to respond.

As I stood in line at the bar, I mentally rehashed everything I knew about the Valencia case. I went through the list of possible suspects and their alibis.

Birdie was the only one whose alibi I wasn't sure about. She said she was at dinner with her husband—but Larry had just revealed he was with Stan that night.

I ducked out of line and went in search of the woman who probably wanted my head on a platter right now.

I found Birdie talking to a couple standing next to an oversized oil painting of a canyon.

"The artist is quite popular here in the southwest region, you know. You almost can't get pieces from him anymore," Birdie was saying to the couple. She waved her red-painted nails toward the painting for effect.

"Excuse me, Birdie, can I talk to you?" I butted in.

Both the man and woman Birdie was talking to shot me a thankful look.

"No," she said pointedly, eyes glued to the painting.

"That's okay, Birdie. We have other paintings to look at," the woman said.

The man agreed. "Yeah, we'll see you around."

The couple walked off quickly and didn't look back.

Birdie whirled on me. "What now? You've implicated me in a murder, convinced my husband to leave me, and humiliated me in the process." Tears streamed down the woman's face, streaking her flawless makeup.

People around us began to stare.

I grabbed Birdie's arm and pulled her into a darkened corner of the room. She didn't fight me. She faced the wall and broke into sobs.

Steeling myself for even louder blubbering, I asked her. "Where were you the night of the murder? For real."

To my surprise, though she continued to sob, her crying didn't get any louder. She sniffed and answered, "I had planned a surprise dinner for Larry at La Fonda. I had the chef prepare all his favorites, you know. Got his favorite wine. Private corner of the restaurant. Private waiter. It took me weeks to arrange it all, but I wanted it to be perfect." Birdie continued to cry and sniffle, but her hysterics were easing up. "I knew he was having an affair. I was trying to win him back. I didn't know he was...I didn't know about Stan. Not until tonight. It explains a lot. But that night...that night I waited for him at the restaurant. But he never came. He said he had to work late. I was humiliated." The loud sobs began again. "I'm always humiliated!"

"Birdie..." I said, gently touching her arm.

She threw her arms around me and cried on my bare shoulder, her body heaving with sobs.

I patted her back. "Birdie, this isn't your fault."

She pulled back and appeared to gain control again. "Of course it's not my fault. When his father introduced us...he said Larry wasn't romantic. That I'd 'have to do the heavy lifting in the romance department.' I don't know if he knew or not. I certainly didn't. Larry *is* romantic. Just not with women."

"But now you'll be free to find someone who is," I said.

Birdie nodded and pulled a tissue out of her small purse. She dabbed at her eyes. "How bad does it look?" she asked me.

"You look like you've been crying. Nothing that a few minutes and a stiff drink won't take care of." I pulled a small mirror out of my equally small purse. "Here," I said, handing it to her.

She cleaned up her makeup as best she could in the dark corner of the ballroom. I looked around and found that no one was staring at us anymore.

"Shall we go get that drink now?" I asked her, pointing to the bar I had just come from.

"Absolutely," she answered without hesitation.

Birdie and I got in line at the bar and made it to the front quickly. We ordered our drinks and stepped aside to wait for them.

"Thank you..." she said, swallowing hard. "...for listening. I haven't been very kind to you. And I don't blame you for thinking I might have killed Mrs. Valencia. That woman and I never saw eye-to-eye." Birdie looked around the room and sighed. "She hated this, you know."

"What do you mean?" I asked.

"I convinced the rest of the board members to put on this huge show, because I knew it would generate a lot more money for our organization, and for the poor, abused women at the shelter. But Eleanor—Mrs. Valencia—always believed art should be an intimate experience. She was furious about this." Birdie laughed.

"She sounds like she had some strong opinions," I said, laughing too. I still didn't trust Birdie's new attitude toward me...but it was nice to have a civil conversation with her.

"Absolutely. Stubborn. Willful. Her son is a lot like her in that—though I think her attitude came from her loss, where his comes more from his profession."

"Ben told me about Teresa's death. So sad." As I said that, the bartender pushed our martinis across the bar to us.

"Where is Ben tonight?" Birdie asked me.

"Working," I said. "He helped me move my things into storage yesterday. I tried to convince him to call in sick and be my plus-one to this event. He didn't go for it." I laughed.

Birdie chuckled. "He wouldn't have gotten away with it. This is a tiny town."

I shrugged. "I'm sure you're right. And it's

probably best anyway. The last thing I need is to get romantically involved..."

Out of the corner of my eye, I saw Aaron stop at a side door, look around to see if anyone was watching, and slip through.

"Birdie, are you going to be okay if I leave you here? There's someone I need to go talk to," I said to the now calm and collected socialite.

"I'm fine. And thank you," Birdie said. "I appreciate your kindness tonight. I won't forget it."

I smiled at my new...friend?...as I walked toward the door where Aaron had just disappeared to.

# CHAPTER
# TWENTY-THREE

---

When my eyes adjusted to the darkened space beyond the side door of the reception hall, I was surprised to see a large room full of cardboard boxes and wooden shipping crates. They were the right shapes and sizes to hold paintings and even some sizeable sculptures, and I wondered if this was additional stock for the SFPAA fundraising event.

I walked further back into the room and noticed an open door on the other side of a six-by-six crate. The room beyond was lit up much brighter than the room I was walking through, and I felt myself drawn to the light like a moth.

I cautiously peered around the door frame. There was nowhere else Aaron could have gone, but the man was nowhere in sight. The smaller, brighter room was also filled with boxes, many of them partially open, revealing paintings within. On the other side of the room was another open door—this one appearing to lead to an alley outside. I made a beeline for the scuffed metal door propped open by a flimsy looking doorstop.

I was almost to the alley when familiar colors caught my eye. Just inside the door was a painting wrapped in several layers of plastic wrap and padded by several sets of foam wedges—and it looked an awful lot like El Camino de Rosas.

*It couldn't be. The Camino is at Villa Valencia.*

I had to move two other boxes out of the way to get close enough to get a better look. The plastic was so thick—while the colors and shapes were identical to the Camino, I wouldn't be able to tell if it was that exact painting unless I could make out the brushstrokes. I looked around the room and my eyes lighted on a box-cutter about five feet away.

"Not so fast," Aaron said, dashing through the door from the alley. He came around the back side of a stack of boxes and grabbed the knife before I could reach it.

I put my hands up, "Whoa there. I was just curious about this painting."

"Curiosity killed the cat, you know. And it's certainly killed you." Aaron sneered. He held the box-cutter assertively, like it was a natural extension of his arm.

Hands still in the air, I tried to look around for something I could use to defend myself without making it obvious. "What are you doing? This isn't funny," I said with mock confidence, worried that my shaking voice gave me away. Just then I saw a hammer on the ground near the painting.

I made a move for the hammer, but Aaron beat me to it, kicking it out of my reach. The metal head made a terrible screeching sound as it scraped across the floor, then a dull thud as it landed against the side of a box.

Defeated, I held my hands up again. "Can we talk about this?" I asked, my heart in my throat.

"I wasn't a murderer," he said. "I *wasn't*. Now...It didn't have to end this way."

"It still doesn't," I started.

"It's too late. The painting is spoken for—and

it's going to pay off a debt to a very dangerous man." Aaron shrugged. "The way I see it, now that you're here, it's my life or yours." He ran his free hand down the front of his suit jacket. "And I like being alive."

Suddenly, Bianca yelled from somewhere behind me. "Hey!"

I turned to look, and Aaron took advantage of the moment to wrap his arm around my throat. He pushed the blade against my cheek.

"Don't make another sound, Bianca," he hissed. "Or your friend's blood will turn this room into a Jackson Pollock painting."

From the angle at which Aaron was holding my head, I could only catch glimpses of Bianca's pained expression. Like me, she had responded to this homicidal art dealer's threats by putting her hands in the air.

Aaron kept the boxcutter pressed tightly against my cheek, and I could feel the blade breaking my skin. "Very slowly, come around and pick up this painting," he ordered. "You're going to put that in my car—and you're going to do it without drawing any attention to us, or your husband's next case will be the murder of his wife and her best friend."

He squeezed my neck with the crook of his elbow and my head was pulled back painfully. I couldn't tell if Bianca had nodded—and she didn't say a word—but I heard the shuffle of feet and the scrape of plastic on cement.

Aaron pulled me roughly across the room and I struggled not to trip and cause him to dig the knife deeper. I could already feel the rush of warm blood running down my jawline and onto my neck. He moved me through the door, into the alley, and over to the side of an SUV with an open trunk.

As he relaxed his grip just a little, I was able to tilt my head down and see Bianca loading the painting into the back of the vehicle. Her hand slipped and the painting landed hard on the floor of the SUV.

"Be careful!" Aaron hissed.

"I'm sorry!" Bianca yelled in a whisper. I could hear the tremor in her voice.

It was just enough of a distraction for him to loosen his grip on me. I twisted out of his grasp, the boxcutter slicing my ear in the process. I cried out sharply.

I expected Aaron to make a grab for me, so I darted out of his reach as quickly as I could, dashing toward Bianca who was still standing behind the SUV. The searing pain of the cut overwhelmed my senses, though, and I overshot her position, nearly slamming into the wall on the other side of the alley.

Aaron grabbed Bianca before I could get to her. He put the knife to her throat.

"Get your hands off her!" I shouted.

"Shut up!" he yelled, digging the tip of the blade into her skin.

Bianca whimpered.

"How did you even know it was me?" he asked, tightening his grip on Bianca's squirming form. "How could *you*, a wannabe artist, figure me out?"

"The varnish was too new," I said with a shrug. "I could smell it. The painting in the Valencia house was a forgery. A really *good* forgery—but still a forgery. That's why you didn't jump on the chance to see if Tom would sell it to you after his mother was murdered."

Out of the corner of my eye, I saw a tire iron tucked to the side of the trunk. I put my hands in the air and moved slowly toward it, keeping my eyes on Aaron.

"Stop moving." he demanded. "I already killed

once—and it was easier than I expected to crack that old woman's head open. I'll kill Bianca too. Don't think I won't."

I lowered my hands slowly and let my right hand rest on the tire iron. I wrapped my fingers around the steel shaft, and, carefully so my movement wouldn't spook Aaron, lifted it over the painting. "You move, I move," I said, raising my hand so Aaron could clearly see the tire iron and its precarious position over the painting in the trunk of the vehicle.

"You wouldn't dare," he sneered.

I felt my body shaking right down to my silver pumps. "Let her go, Aaron," I said as coolly as I could.

For what felt like minutes, but was probably only seconds, Aaron and I stared at each other unflinching.

Aaron squeezed Bianca's neck harder and she gasped.

I raised the tire-iron higher.

"Freeze!" Rocky yelled from the doorway we had just exited. He was backlit by the fluorescent light of the reception hall storage room, but his stance indicated he was holding a gun pointed straight at Aaron's head—and, unfortunately, Bianca's.

Aaron's dark eyes flitted from me to Rocky, then to the driver's side door of the SUV. His body language broadcast his next move and I had a split second to decide how I was going to react.

Aaron shoved Bianca toward Rocky, effectively creating a human shield. I dropped the tire iron and made a grab for her, yanking her across the alley with me to give Rocky a clear shot. Rocky fired at Aaron's fleeing form, hitting the open driver's side door as Aaron ducked into the SUV. In the three seconds it took Aaron to put his key in the ignition, start the engine, and put the vehicle in drive, Rocky fired his gun two more times.

Bianca and I clung to each other against the wall of the alley opposite from Rocky. I saw Aaron's body slump in the driver's seat on the third shot.

The SUV rolled slowly down the alley, coming to rest against a dumpster.

# CHAPTER TWENTY-FOUR

Most of the partygoers had gone home, and Bianca and I were left in the ballroom with a variety of law enforcement professionals all peppering us with questions. I couldn't understand why they were asking us many of the *same* questions. Couldn't they just all stand in one place and get the information from us at one time?

My head was spinning, my cheek was burning, and my ear was throbbing where a paramedic had stitched the deeper cut. Bianca hadn't left Rocky's arms since the moment he put down his gun in the alley and called in the incident.

Rocky's commanding officer had assured us that Rocky wasn't going to be facing murder charges. A vehicle can be a weapon, and Aaron was about to use that weapon in a situation where he'd already threatened two people's lives.

I wasn't sad that Aaron had died. Maybe I should have been—he was a human being, after all. But I couldn't muster the sympathy.

My heart broke, however, when the forensic team announced that the painting had been damaged beyond repair.

One of the genius Navarro's priceless masterworks had been demolished—and I was responsible. When I dropped the tire iron, the claw gouged the exposed portion of the canvas. Then when the SUV hit the dumpster, the tire iron ripped a huge gash across the painting.

El Camino de Rosas was irreparable.

"What I don't understand," I said to Rocky, "is Aaron's alibi. He was seen on camera hanging paintings at a gallery when Mrs. Valencia was killed."

A crease appeared between Rocky's brows. "That's bothering me, too. I haven't seen the footage myself—the investigators were the ones who confirmed Aaron's alibi. I'll get my hands on that video as soon as possible and see what answers I can get."

I saw Birdie push through the throng of law enforcement professionals and make a beeline for me. I steeled myself for another dramatic display.

"I'm so glad you're okay!" she said as she threw her arms around me.

Bianca gave me a confused look. I mouthed *"Tell you later"* over Birdie's bony shoulder.

"It was scary. And the Navarro painting is damaged beyond repair. So I don't feel quite *okay* yet..." I started.

"The Camino?" Birdie gasped. She stepped back and put her long-fingered hand over her mouth.

"Yeah. It's gone."

"What was it doing here? Why wasn't it at Villa Valencia?" Birdie's eyes welled up as she spoke.

"I didn't know you were an art lover," I said, shocked at her reaction.

"Well that's just silly. Why do you think I'm on the board of the SFPAA?" Birdie's voice went up an octave.

"I thought it was just a...social thing, I guess." I said.

"Fun fact about Birdie Lemon," she said, a smile

creeping over her red lips. "I have a master's degree in art history."

My jaw dropped. "You continue to surprise me," I said when I'd regained my composure. "To answer your question, Aaron stole the Camino from Mrs. Valencia's house when he murdered her, and replaced it there with the forgery—and I'm pretty sure he has been hiding the original here in the stock room for safekeeping since then."

Birdie nodded. "That makes sense, I suppose. As much as anything makes sense tonight."

"Birdie, out of curiosity, what was it that you and Stan were up to? When I overheard you in Bianca's boutique..."

"You mean when you were spying on us," Birdie corrected. She crossed her arms delicately and raised an eyebrow at me.

"Okay. When we were *gathering intel*," I said with a laugh, "Stan said you 'made Mrs. Valencia pay.' What was that about?"

Birdie took a deep breath. "I'm not proud of this," she said. "If I had known how things would end up for her...Well, Stan found a forensic accountant and I paid him to find...missteps in Mrs. Valencia's tax records. Anomalies that we could threaten to report to the IRS if she ever tried to sell the Villa Valencia property to someone other than me." Birdie looked at her feet.

"Ah," I said. "That explains it."

Birdie was all but knocked out of the way when Ben came barreling through the bustling ballroom. Without saying a word, he tackled me in a giant bear hug.

"Whoa there!" I said as I hugged him back.

Ben didn't respond. He just kept squeezing me.

"I'm okay," I whispered into his ear.

He squeezed harder.

Moments later, he finally released his embrace. He kept his hands on my upper arms and looked me squarely in the eyes as he stood back. He took a deep breath and squared his shoulders, his fraught expression revealed both relief and worry.

"You're okay," he said.

"I'm okay," I repeated.

Looking past him, I saw Rocky and Bianca watching us with matching amusement. Bianca had her head on Rocky's shoulder.

Ben turned and waved them both over. "You'll want to hear this," he said. "We found David Ramirez. He was caught in a sting trying to buy forged documents for three of his cousins. He tried to make a run for it, and one of my guys got swept up in the chase on the highway. It was the most exciting thing to happen all day—big story in District 1."

"Wait a minute," Rocky said. He let go of Bianca's hand and pulled his cell phone out of his inside jacket pocket. "Were these the cousins?" He turned the phone so Ben could see the same photo Rocky had sent me earlier of the three drivers licenses he found near Kathy's body.

"Yeah, that's them."

"Kathy was a forger," Rocky said with certainty. "That would explain the documents we found at the scene. I wonder...Hang on." He ducked away and left Bianca standing alone.

Ben didn't let her stand alone for long. He took the opportunity to wrap her in a long bear hug too.

"Did I hear someone mention forgery?" A short woman in cat-eye glasses walked up. She extended her hand to me. "I'm Angela, a forensic art investigator. They called me up from Albuquerque as an extra set of eyes, since this case is so...unusual."

"Unusual?" I asked. Everything about this felt

unusual to me, but I wondered what made it unusual to an investigator like her.

"The Santa Fe police department's go-to art consultant is the deceased suspect. Yeah, unusual." She frowned. "I overheard you talking about forgery. Do you know something about the painting?"

"I know the painting in Eleanor Valencia's house, the supposed El Camino de Rosas by Alejandro Navarro, is a forgery. I could smell the varnish on it," I said confidently.

Angela's frown deepened. "Come here for a moment." She crooked her finger at me and I followed her back through the side door to the storage room.

My flesh crawled with goosebumps walking back toward the place where Bianca and I almost died. Luckily, I didn't have to go too far into that room. Angela had the torn Navarro painting laying on top of a makeshift easel she created out of stacked boxes.

"Is this the painting you were talking about?" she asked, pointing at the shredded masterpiece.

My eyes welled. "No," I said, turning away.

"That's the real painting that I accidentally destroyed."

Angela shook her head. "It's a forgery."

"Excuse me?" I said, my mouth falling open.

"Look here." She pointed at the torn edge of the canvas.

"It's...it's too thin to be a Navarro piece. He used three layers of gesso. This painting has no more than one layer." I ran my fingers along the tattered edge.

In a flash, it came together in my head.

"They're both forgeries." I whispered to no one in particular. I whirled on Angela. "So then where's the original?"

"You tell me," she said, her arms crossed.

"How would I know?"

"You seem to know a lot."

"If I knew where the original Camino was, it would be on its way to a museum right now." I crossed my arms too.

"Break it up, you two," Rocky said as he walked in the room. "Angela, Ali is good people. And she almost died tonight protecting this painting. Give her a break." He turned to me. "Can I have a word with you?"

I followed Rocky back out into the main ballroom. He guided me to a secluded corner behind an abandoned (but still well-stocked) bar. He made eye contact with Ben and waved him over as well.

"I just got off the phone with the coroner," he said as Ben walked up. "Toxicology came back. Kathy died of a drug overdose."

"Oh," I said, not knowing exactly how to respond.

"It wasn't a...suicide?" Ben asked. His hazel eyes looked like they may burst with tears at any moment.

"No, Ben. It wasn't a suicide." Rocky patted his friend's shoulder. He turned to me. "The belt we found at the scene—the one you said looked like David's—she was using it as a tourniquet. She stole it from an unlocked car nearby. It wasn't David's."

"Oh," I said again.

"Evidence suggests she was a professional forger and David hired her to create documentation for his relatives who came into this country illegally. They found more forged documents at the hostel she was staying at. They weren't top quality, but they'd pass quick inspection."

Rocky rocked back on his heels, his hands in his pockets. He looked at me expectantly.

"And..." I prompted, not sure what he wanted me to say.

"Kathy was a forger. We have two forged Navarro paintings. This all seems pretty tidy to me. She scammed Mrs. Valencia and Aaron both."

I shook my head. "No. There's no way. You said the documents she forged weren't top quality? These forged paintings were *impeccable*." I put my hands on my hips.

Rocky shrugged. "Well, the investigators will get to the bottom of it. But I think we've nailed our murderer *and* our forger tonight."

I nodded uneasily, feeling like there was still a puzzle piece missing.

# CHAPTER TWENTY-FIVE

I stood in the doorway of the little house and sighed as I surveyed the empty rooms. *This is it. The perfect launching pad for my artist career here in Santa Fe...no longer mine. I hope I find something else even half this wonderful.*

Larry had kept his word. He sent his assistant Maggie over that morning with a check for half the cost of the commissioned portrait. It was enough for a down payment on a new place here in Santa Fe, and a couple of months of expenses.

Rocky informed me that paint chips from my Jeep were found on the tire iron in the trunk of Aaron's SUV. Though there was no way to prove it, all signs pointed to Aaron being the one who gouged the side of my Jeep in the parking garage downtown.

Bianca and Rocky invited me to crash on their couch and use their garage as a makeshift studio while I looked for a new place. While I appreciated their offer, and immediately took them up on it, I was anxious to find a place of my own. I was also anxious to sleep in my own bed again—their couch was murder on my back.

My start in Santa Fe was a rough one. But I had a start. I was happy with that.

The two house keys jangled in my hand as I wound my way through the still-flourishing garden to the back door of the main house.

Tom opened the door before I could knock. He leaned on the doorframe, arms crossed. His beady eyes looked slightly less beady—but maybe I was seeing him through the eyes of nostalgia for my first home in Santa Fe.

"What do you want?" he said gruffly.

I held my hand out and presented him with the keys to the Little House.

He simply stared at me and shook his head.

"Take them, Tom. Don't make this any more difficult." I pushed the keys toward him.

He shook his head again. "You did it," he said. "You figured out who murdered my mother. I don't know how...but you did it."

"Yeah. And I was nearly killed in the process. Happy?"

The corners of Tom's mouth pulled down into a half frown. "Look...we don't have to be friends. But we don't have to be enemies either. I appreciate what you did. You can stay. I'll let you keep the lease as-is for a year. Then we'll renegotiate."

For the first time since I arrived in Santa Fe, I couldn't hold back the tears. I could feel my face crumbling, and I held my hands up to cover up the sight.

Tom reached out and patted me on the shoulder. "You're welcome."

I looked up through parted fingers. "You are such a JERK!" I shouted. "You couldn't have told me that before I put all of my worldly belongings in storage?"

Tom doubled over with laughter. "Now I'm happy," he said through bouts of laughter. "Now we're even!"

We both pulled ourselves together. I swiped the back of my hand across my cheeks and giggled when I saw how much mascara had streaked down my face.

"Welcome to New Mexico," Tom said, once again leaning on the doorframe. "I really do wish you luck here."

I nodded. As I turned to go call Bianca and tell her the good news (well, good news for me—but she was going to be upset that I wasn't crashing on her couch anymore), Tom called for me to come back.

"Come in here a minute," he said, pointing toward the living room.

I followed him into the main house. The living room looked bare without the large painting above the fireplace.

In the corner, propped up against the arm of a well-worn leather couch was a collection of at least half a dozen paintings. Tom slid one of the canvases out of the stack and held it up. "I found these in my mother's storage unit," he said. "Do they look familiar?"

"They're...they're Navarros," I said, inching closer. I touched the canvas, pushing gently to feel the thickness. I ran my fingertips over the paint, then I tilted my head to look across the surface. "Wait, no. They're not. They're more forgeries."

"Yeah. That's what the art authenticator said too," Tom said. He put the painting back in the front of the stack, then ran his hand over his balding head. "I think my mother was forging artwork."

I pinched my lips together and let out a breath through my nose. "Kathy was forging documents. Your mother was forging paintings. What are the chances that they..."

"Were partners? And had a falling out?" Tom nodded. "My thought exactly. It would explain why Kathy suddenly reneged on our deal."

"And poor Aaron thought he was pulling one over on your mother," I said with a laugh. "She was a much better forger than he was." I shook my head. "Your mother was an interesting woman."

Tom smiled at me, his expression wistful. "Yes, she was."

"And Aaron was a weasel."

"Yes, he was."

"He blackmailed David Ramirez, you know."

Tom's mouth dropped open. "Blackmailed? Over what?"

"Aaron found out David had purchased fake documents for his cousins," I explained, "and he used that information to blackmail David into going to the gallery the night of the murder. It was David on the video from the gallery—not Aaron."

"The two men look nothing alike..." Tom started.

"Aaron coached him on how to avoid the camera as much as possible, and to keep his face hidden completely." I shrugged. "At least, that's what he confessed when Rocky looked closely at the video and figured out it was David."

"What a mess," Tom said. He put his hands in the pockets of his khakis. "Murders, forgeries, bribery...even my worst day in court was never this messy."

"Speaking of messy, did you ever find out who ransacked your Santa Fe office?" I asked.

Tom chuckled. "It's not nearly as sinister as the rest of this situation turned out to be. Someone had broken in and was living in the building. My guess is he was looking for something valuable in the files while he was there—checks, maybe."

"Yeah, that's almost a letdown after all of this," I joked. It felt good to have a normal conversation with Tom. One that didn't end up in yelling, name calling, or slamming doors. I took a deep breath and said, "Thanks for letting me stay here, Tom."

"You're welcome," he said with the kindest smile I'd seen yet. "Don't trash it."

# CHAPTER TWENTY-SIX

_____

The wind whipped through my newly colored hair as I looked out over the edge of the Rio Grande Gorge. The early September sun warmed my arms as they rested on top of the split-rail fence that separated the trail from the chasm.

Ben stood next to me, his arm around my shoulders. "Thanks for coming with me," he said.

I nodded. "Of course." I shivered as Ben ran his fingers through my now cotton-candy pink locks.

"How is Larry's portrait going?"

I beamed. "It's great. He's a really fun subject to paint." I snapped my fingers. "Oh! I almost forgot to tell you, Felicia found a buyer for a series of paintings that I did back in Chicago."

"The ones of the guys in suits?"

"No," I said, shaking my head. "These were still-life paintings of flowers."

"Flowers? I thought you only painted portraits."

I laughed. "You have a lot to learn about me," I said, grinning sideways at the handsome officer.

Small white clouds danced in the azure sky above the deep gorge. What little I could see of the water below was white and churning.

"This place is the beginning and end of stories," Ben said after a few moments of silence. "Teresa's story ended here. My story began." He put his hand on my waist and squeezed lightly. "Thank you for coming with me today. I've been wanting to come back here for years—ever since I heard they'd finally put up a fence. You know, just to honor Teresa's memory. I was never brave enough."

I tilted my head to look at Ben's lightly tanned face, his well-defined jaw soft with the emotion of the moment. My instincts had been wrong about Alex—and on top of it, I missed all the obvious warning signs that he wasn't who I thought he was. Could I trust my instincts now? Could I trust myself to see Ben for who he was?

I had stopped by the Desert Wind Boutique

earlier that morning to visit Bianca. "You've got friends here, now," she said to me. "Family, even, if you want it."

Her words echoed in my mind as I stood with Ben in that moment and helped him face his own past mistakes.

"I see another new beginning starting here today." I said, smiling up at those hazel eyes. The smell of warm sagebrush wafted past my nose. It smelled like home.

# About the Author

Jessica Mehring is a Colorado-based author, copywriter and entrepreneur. She believes that history and nature are our greatest teachers, yet she is also endlessly fascinated by technology and the human brain. She loves reading, walks in the woods, yoga, and creating and collecting art. She lives with her husband, two daughters, and one spoiled mutt — and her growing collection of books and office supplies are slowly taking over their house.

You can connect with Jessica at jessicamehringauthor.com.